XANDER

WINCHESTER BROTHERS BOOK 4

KATHI S. BARTON

This is a work of fiction. Names, characters, places, and incidents are products of the author's imagination or are used fictitiously and are not to be construed as real. Any resemblance to actual events, locations, organizations, or persons, living or dead, is entirely coincidental.

World Castle Publishing, LLC
Pensacola, Florida

Copyright © Kathi S. Barton 2018
Paperback ISBN: 9781629899480
eBook ISBN: 9781629899497
First Edition World Castle Publishing, LLC, July 9, 2018
http://www.worldcastlepublishing.com

Licensing Notes

Cover: Karen Fuller
Editor: Maxine Bringenberg

Prologue

Tyler saw his big brother coming toward him. Xander hadn't seen him yet, which was okay with him. Xander would probably just walk away and go someplace else where Tyler wasn't. Not just with Tyler, but everybody. He'd been like that since Wendy had died. She'd been his mate.

"You gonna talk to me?" Xander stopped and said that he didn't want to talk to anyone. "No, I guess you made that kind of clear. I'm worried about you. Everybody is."

"I'm all right. It's a big blow to my heart, even though I didn't know her at all." She'd been killed when someone raided the store she'd been in with her momma, killing them both as well as several other people there. "When we were at the funeral, Dad had to help me away, do you remember that? I sort of feel like that all the time now. Broken."

"Yes, we all do. Dad said that she didn't suffer any. I don't understand people, Xander. To kill anyone, that's so sad, but to do it for nothing more than because they didn't have the

5

right kind of honey for his cereal is just plain stupid."

Xander sat down next to him. "I could smell her, even with all those chemicals. But I knew right then what she was to me."

"I don't know what I'd do if that happened to me. Dad said you wasn't taking it hard then, but you seem to be now." Xander nodded. "I guess you had time to think on it, huh?"

"Yeah. Mom and Dad, they got it right, you know that? They tell each other all the time that they love each other. I was gonna do that too." Tyler didn't know why people would even like a girl, much less love one, but he did agree that his parents were mushy like that. "I'll never get to have a kid of my own either. Not that I want one right now, but I thought that someday I'd want one. A whole bunch of them that I could play with, like Dad did us."

"I don't ever want to have any sons, Xander. Boys are all I have right now in brothers." Xander ruffled up his hair, like he always did. "Someday I guess I might want sons, but you guys are always being bossy and stuff. I hate that."

"We're just trying to make sure that you do things right, little brother."

Tyler nodded and thought of all the things that had been going on of late. "You know, Mr. Cartwright, he told me that someday, I was going to think back on him and wonder why he'd been wanting to be a part of our family. I told him that I knew why. My momma baked the best pies in the world."

"She does at that. But I don't think he does it for that reason. He's lonely and sad sometimes, have you noticed that? Anyway, I think that he comes over not for the food, but because we're nice to him. And he's nice to us." Xander laid back on the ground. "I'm about done being mopey, as Mom called me. I just had it hit me what all I was going to miss. But, I guess that's the way the fates wanted it. Come on, let's go and get us some dinner. Mom said we're having the catfish that you and Mr. Cartwright caught yesterday."

Tyler didn't care all that much for catfish, but he knew better than to turn down meat. They didn't have it often — sometimes they'd go a whole week without any. But when they did have it, they ate it like it was gold filled. Being wolves, they needed it. But there was usually plenty of other stuff to go with it, and Mom always had some hot bread to fill up the voids when there were any. There might not be tonight. He'd caught ten catfish yesterday and Mr. Cartwright had caught himself a dozen, then handed them over to Tyler to give to his momma to cook up.

Xander walked alongside of him, shortening his steps so that he could keep up. Tyler had all these dreams of somedays. That's what he called his list, Somedays. Someday he was going to have it all too.

Someday he was going to have a nice car. Not new — they weren't worth the payments, Dad said. Someday he was going to own him a house. Really close to his parents, he decided just then. Someday he was going to be rich too. Just so he could make it easier on his mom and dad. Someday, he thought lastly, he was going to meet him a nice girl, even though he didn't like them, and have him a bunch of kids. Someday. Not now, but someday.

"Do you suppose that the fates — or whatever it is that sets us up like this — you suppose that they take in account that your mate might have something happen to him or her?"

There were times, like at this moment, that Tyler thought his older brother was too young for his brain. "You know what I mean, don't you?"

"Yes, I understand you. But I honestly don't know, Xander. I mean, they know everybody's fate. You know, that's their name, right? I would think that they'd know that from the minute they set you up." He didn't think that was nice, so Tyler tried to fix it. "But I'm only a kid and you're almost a big adult. Well, you are big. Like big-headed. Big footed. What sized shoe do you wear now? Or do you just go on out to the field and kick two cows in the bottom and wear them?"

Tyler wasn't stupid nor was he very fast, but they took off running as soon as his brother growled. Laughing too hard to go far, he felt his brother's big wolf take him down and lick him all over his face. They were having so much fun, he'd forgotten why Xander had come to find him in the first place. It was dinner time.

It was always nice having Mr. Cartwright over. He always brought a treat, as he called it. Sometimes it was the stuff to make ice cream. Other times it was just a big cake that had been on sale or something. Tyler thought the man was just being nice. He'd been in the store a lot with his momma and hadn't ever seen a sale on those sized cakes. But he ate whatever it was because it was always good.

"Mr. Cartwright won't be joining us tonight, sons." He asked his dad why not. "Well, today was the date that his wife passed on, and he goes and sits with her for a spell." Tyler glanced at Xander but said nothing.

"Why don't we gather up some of those flowers that are gonna die anyway and take them over to her grave for him?"

Caleb always had the best ideas. Tyler wished he had one or two like he did. "We don't have to stay, just show him that we care that he's hurting."

"Wonderful idea, Caleb." Tyler wanted to kick his brother under the table, but he'd not do that again. He would make him pay later. Almost as if he knew what he was thinking, Caleb stabbed him with his eyes.

Caleb was the oldest, and sometimes when he was being big brother, he'd just beat him to a pulp for the fun of it. Not really. Tyler would sort of make him mad, just to see him running after him. Caleb was the best big brother there was.

They took the flowers to Mrs. Cartwright's grave and were invited to stay by Mr. Cartwright. But Mom said they had supper on and wouldn't be bothering him. Mr. Cartwright kissed his fingers and laid them on top of the pretty headstone that Dad had helped carve, and said he'd join them.

"The time for mourning is done. I have to.... It'll be easier with you guys around, but I have to stop acting like I'm gonna come out here and she's going to be waiting on me."

Dad told him that they'd be powerful sorry if he went with her. Tyler had no idea what that meant, but he wisely kept his mouth shut. Grownups were touchy about death, love, and such.

That night when he and Dominic were in their room, he asked him what he thought about what Xander had said — about there being someone else out there for him. Then he told him what he'd told his brother.

"I think that's what Mom would call you being insensitive, moron." He asked him how. "Because that was the time when a little fib would have made him feel better. You know, like when Mom asks us if she looks tired and she does, but we all tell her that she's right pretty."

"But that's not the kind of question that Xander asked me. He wanted to know the truth." Or he had thought he did. "I did try and tell him that I was only just a kid. And him being an almost adult."

"There. See? You did it twice. You called him almost an adult. He's not an adult and saying almost only makes it sound like you don't think he's going to ever be. I swear, there are some times, Tyler, that I think you were born under a rock or something." He pointed out to his brother he was being insensitive too. "Yeah? Well, think how that made you feel."

For the rest of the night he did think about how it made him feel. Nothing. They were always calling him a moron, or something like that. Instead of thinking of it as a bad thing, Tyler thought of it as a learning curve. Yeah, he did learn that he was a might on the insensitive side. But his brothers were older than him, except Dominic, and the two of them needed to grow some.

Not that he was sure what they were supposed to grow, but he'd heard that at the high school a few weeks back and was glad now that he'd found a way to use it. But, like the rest of them, he'd never say something like that, or curse in front of their mom. She was scary when she was upset about something.

Chapter 1

Addie wasn't sure how she'd been moved. She did know where she was, which had come to her when she'd rolled over and seen the pretty woman sleeping in the chair next to her. There wasn't any way that she'd moved — The air was suddenly perfumed with her scent. A breeding wolf.

I thought it best that no one could tell what you were. She thanked Bug for helping her in that. *They have a lot of questions, but they have said nothing to anyone in their family. And they are a large and tight knit group. The older brother, he is the pack master.*

What do you know of what happened to me? There has to be a reason that the FBI was out to try and kill me when they're the ones that hired me in the first place. He said that he was checking into that now. *Good. Also, I would like you to find my boss. See what you can find out. I need to know what he did or didn't do to get me shot to fuck.*

I will leave now to find out. I was staying with you in case you might need me for something. She said that she was fine now that she was awake. *The drugs they are giving you, you should take them for today. They're helping you rest, and that can only be good when you're so hurt. I don't think anyone knows where you are, but you must be well enough to defend these people if they do.*

I'll think on that.

He knew as well as she that the drugs were finished. As she told Bug, she was awake now and would be fine. When he flew from her body, she looked at the woman and saw that she was awake and staring at her. Addie started to rise when she told her not to move just yet.

"There are some stitches in your belly that are going to be pulled again if you jerk around. You've already had to have them replaced once. And Gabe is visiting patients right now, so he can't come home to keep you together. The bullets have all been removed, and they're in the safe should you ever want or need them." Addie sat up, slowly, with the woman's assistance. "Thank you. I wasn't sure if you'd pull a weapon on me. You and I talked, do you remember that? It was in the alley where you were hurt. Gabe is my husband, and he's a doctor."

"You know who I work for then. I'm assuming that someone told you?" The woman, she thought her name was Rayne, nodded and said that somehow, it had come to them. Much like them coming to her aid had. "You're not just a breeding wolf either, are you?"

"No, I'm not." Nothing else, but since Addie did the same thing when she didn't know someone, she let it go. For now, anyway. "No one knows where you are. I'm sure that your sigil told you that. Does it have a name?"

"Bug. And it's a male. Counterbalance and all." She

nodded. "You're Rayne. There's something more, but I can't touch it right now. But I will. Or you could just tell me, and I'd have it."

"Death watcher." She stood up and stretched, like telling someone that she was the death watcher wasn't such a big deal. "You have many ghosts with you, did you know that? None of them mean you bad will, but I can help them if you'd allow it. And in a way, I believe that they have helped you. Or, and I'm guessing here, you never would have made it this long in your life.

"I have, thank you. What the hell are you doing here?" She just smiled. "I hate coy people. Just cut the shit and tell me what I'm doing in the house of a breeding wolf that claims she's the death watcher."

Before she could stand, if she was going to do something, she was lifted from the bed and held up by her throat, which was being closed off. As soon as Rayne looked her in the eyes, she could see that she was indeed the death watcher, and she wasn't one to fuck with either. Being let go, Addie landed on the side of the bed and sat there. That was one scary bitch.

"Don't forget it either. Now, as I was saying, you have several ghosts with you. Some of them are just hanging around to help in case you didn't know that. And two of them are stuck with you. I can assist them in moving on, but I think that would be up to you." She asked who they were. "One says his name is Pierson, the other is Rankin. He says that he's your mate."

"He wishes. No, neither of them needs to be here." When Rayne looked as if she was listening to someone, Addie stood up again and called to Bug. He'd help her heal, and the sooner

13

she got out of here, the better for everyone. "Rankin said that you have two people that are out to kill you. They're going to your lair today. They will not find anything there, he said—he's had someone take care of it."

"He's a demigod." Rayne sat down when she did. "You're very bitchy. Is it the kid you're carrying? I can tell you right now that it's strong and doing very well."

"No. I just.... What do you know of the death watcher? I mean, other than the monster stories that you might have been told. I can tell that—I know that you're an ancient. Probably as old as all of us put together. So, what might you know that I don't?" She asked if she was new to the job. "No. I've been around for a while. Not as long as you have—I don't think there would be many that have been—but I don't know a lot about myself. Like you, I was chosen—created, if you wish to call it that."

"You're never going to die. Neither will your mate." She said that she'd been told that by a vampire. "She's wrong if she thinks that she gave you that gift. Or curse, depends on how you look at it. You can step down from your job. But as soon as you do, all, and I mean all the creatures, humans and shifters, that you've ever had contact with will die with you. I'll make sure of it. And if you want to know why, I'll tell you now. You'd still have all the powers that you have now. Sending others away, killing if you should need to, as well as true immortality. And that means even a bullet to the heart, removing your head? Those will not work. Nothing that means to kill you can penetrate your flesh. You'll bleed if sliced, but never to the point of death. Only the sword of my body can kill you."

The blade was small when she reached behind her neck and pulled it free. But as they both watched, not only did it lengthen, but it widened as well, like a claymore, its weight and girth so large that in order to use it, Addie would need both hands. But once it was swung, whomever was close would have their bodies sliced in half, or heads removed, whatever it took for them to be dead.

"I was told that when we brought you here. Wally, he's my contact with the other world, he said that I should stab you in your rest and be done with you." She didn't say anything. It might have been something she'd have done too, given the chance. "But, I'd never do that to you. I couldn't take a life unless it meant risking my own, or those of my child or my family. And you don't have to worry about me stepping down. I really do enjoy helping the dead. Well, most of the time I enjoy it. The third person with you is one of the men you killed the other day. He's still unsure what you were targeted for. He's military or some branch that you might be with. Feds, I'm thinking."

"He is. And I don't know either. But having me here, it's going to cause you guys some issues." She said they were used to those. "I'm working for the CIA for the moment. And the man with me, he's FBI. If he doesn't know, then I certainly don't know why I was targeted either. But they were ready for me, to the point of waiting until I did my job before they tried to kill me."

"He said that you killed Boone. That alone will get you major brownie points from this family. We're not involved with him—he's just been a pain in the ass for so long." Addie stood up again, feeling better by the minute. When Rayne asked her if she was hungry, Addie, for some reason, thought it was more of a "You're going to eat" rather than a question of whether she was hungry. Nodding at her, Rayne laughed. "Lunch is ready when you are. There are some clothes in the bathroom that I can only assume your sigil brought you. Down the hall to the left, then at the bottom of the stairs, to the right. You'll be able to smell where we are from there."

When she was alone, Addie went to the bathroom, where she found a stack of clothes; jeans and a T-shirt, a sweat shirt, as well as socks and shoes. She looked at the panties that were there and decided that they were not brought by Bug. He knew that she liked the feel of men's boxer briefs. Using a bit of her magic, she changed them and turned on the water. She really did need to get going.

The shower felt like heaven. As she let the water roll over her battered body, she felt the moment that Bug joined her. He would not come to her body while she was under the water—he was terrified of it for some reason—but he would talk to her.

I've found your boss, my lady. He is dead. Along with two others that you had contact with. They were killed separately; Agent Conair was found dead in his bed beside his wife. They're saying heart attack, but I can smell that it was poison. And the younger man, I forget his name, he was killed in a car accident late last night. She told him his name. *Yes, Cody. The third man, Farquhar, he was found with a rope around his neck and a note saying that he couldn't live with himself any longer. The news reports of his death are saying that he was distraught over having pornography on his computer. It is unclear if it was male or female, but it wasn't children.*

What are they saying about me? He didn't answer, and she finished up her shower — it was spoiled now — and looked at him. *Tell me, Bug. I can't fight if I don't know what's going on.*

It's going around that you went off on your own to kill a person by the name of Westlake. I have a search on him, but all I'm finding is a young man by the same name, and he isn't dead. Before you ask, yes, he is in hiding too. I don't know why they would say such a thing, but I've taken precautions. She asked him how. *The restaurant cameras have been destroyed, as have the ones outside of it and in the surrounding area, to make sure that neither you nor the Winchesters were seen. Also, you should be aware that you are staying in the home of the death watcher and her mate.*

She told me. Turning to get dressed, she pulled on her clothing, then had to undress when she'd forgotten, in her haste, to put on her bra and underwear. *Where is Cate?*

Cate is on a holiday and will not be returning for some time, miss. But she has been warned to be on the lookout. She nodded. *Do they have any idea who you are, my lady? I didn't tell them, but if you know who they are, surely you've told them what you are.*

I didn't have to do that either. Rayne knew. Make sure.... She thought of what was going on and who might be involved. It was too mind boggling to think of how many people could be out to get her.

Bug moved around the countertop. His crawling would set her on edge when she was thinking, and he seemed to remember that when he suddenly stopped. *My lady, you think they know your body then?*

More than likely. As I said, she knows what I am. Nodding, he flew through the air and landed on her shoulder. *Bug, you have to be safe as well. Without you, I'm as good as toast.*

17

As am I, if anything were to happen to you.

They were a pair. Paired as a single person so long ago, she didn't remember the ritual, nor did she remember the names or faces of those that had done it. What she did remember was that Cate was her only weaponry, and Bug kept her safe. When he burrowed under her skin and became the necklace again, she made her way down the stairs to the kitchen. There were several people there, only one that she knew.

"This is my father-in-law, Kelley Winchester, and his mate, Sara. From right to left, Gabe, my mate, Owen, and Dominic, both my brothers-in-law. You can trust them as well as you can trust me." She could have been flippant and told her that she didn't trust her, but didn't. Instead, she sat at the table and was astonished to see all her favorite foods set before her. "This is Abby Snow, the cook. She's a snow cat. The only one left of her kind as a shifter. She will be here all the time to feed you what and when you wish. If you would only give her a moment or two, she can get anything you can think of. She wants you as healthy as we do."

Looking up at the cook, Abby, she was told, Addie thanked her. A full glass was put in front of her, as well as a gallon jug of what appeared to be orange juice. It was fresh too; she could see the pulp settling along the top of the jug as the liquid calmed down enough to separate.

"I know a bit about your kind, miss. Thank you for being here." She nodded and glanced at the doctor and Rayne. "You will come to care for them both too. They're a bit on the mushy side, what with the baby coming and all, but they're a nice, hard-working family. The mister and missus, they did a good job raising their boys up to be good men."

"You're a nice person yourself, Abby. Now, I'm Kelley, as you heard. What I want to know is if any that crap they're saying in the paper is true. So's you know, there aren't any pictures of you. A blurred one, but you can't tell if it's you or me." He laughed, and she smiled at him. "Also, you got nothing to worry about around here. There ain't a soul here that will say a word. We got your back. My son, Caleb—he's the pack leader—he's got the pack keeping an eye out for anything that might come around."

"My back doesn't need for you all to get yourself killed." He nodded and wrapped his arms around his mate. Love. Something that she knew would never be hers. "You seem like a really nice family, but you have no idea what I might be up against."

"Nope, we don't. But that won't stop us from helping you as best we can. We've been hiding out the women of this family since they been coming around. You won't be any different. And if'n you happen to be the mate to one of my sons, the more the merrier." She stood up and Kelley smiled. "You're a might on the big side—tall, I mean—but we got sons that'll match up to you, should you be inclined, I mean."

"Kelley, you should just be quiet now. You're making it sound like you're selling her our sons." He said he wasn't doing that, and that she knew it. "Does she? Well, I'm not so sure. But hush now. She's got things to tell us, and we'll all have some dinner tonight. That way she doesn't have to explain her story to us over and over. You'll be there. At six, at my home."

When she left, Addie looked at the two people that lived there. "What just happened? I get the feeling that even if there were other plans, they've just been canceled." They both laughed, and Addie did as well. "I guess that means I'm going to dinner then. It might be a good thing, I guess. To be able to tell them what to watch for, who might be hanging around and what to do."

"Yes, it is. And if you have nothing to wear, I have something for you. What you have on, that's fine, but I didn't know your plans for the day." Addie nodded at Rayne and told her that she was fine. "Good. I'll be back at five. If you need me, Abby can call me. Or you. Whatever you need."

~*~

Xander was waiting on his publisher to read the final chapter in his book. There was another book that he was writing too, but for now, no one but him knew about it. It was brewing, something that he'd been calling the thoughts that he was putting together for another chapter—or in this case, another book.

"May I ask you a question?" He nodded at Doris Martin, his publisher. "What did you use for your inspiration? I mean, you told me when you first started this book that it was going to be a manual, something to do with farms and starting out. Then a few weeks ago, you told me that you changed your mind and that now you had a different idea, and then started sending me this. And Christ, Xander, have you ever left your seat since you started on this? You've written a book in less than a week."

"Do you not like it?" She laughed. "Look, I know that it wasn't your idea to work with me. That you were probably paid a great deal of money to take me on as a client and to sell my book someplace. I know that. But I don't—"

20

"You're right, you don't. I was asked, as a personal favor to a very nice older gentleman, to let you work with me. Mr. Cartwright told me that you were green but that you had a hidden talent waiting to be tapped. He said that you'd be easy going, that I'd need to shake up your world to get the book, the one he knew was there, to come out. But I didn't have to do that." She picked up the manuscript and waved it in front of her face like an oversized fan. "This is amazing, Xander. I don't mean like really good, but a-fucking-mazing. I expected it to be dry and without form. You gave me humor and a flowing story that makes me want more. A great deal more. And as for typos or even grammar mistakes, there are few of those either. I could take this to the printer right now and have them make a million copies, and it would still sell out."

"A million…. Good joke. But I loved writing this." She said it showed. "I don't want you to sell this, or to say anything to me that you wouldn't say to someone else, please? I want to do this on my own merit. My own works, not just because a nice man asked you to watch over me."

Instead of saying anything to him, she bellowed—actually bellowed—for her secretary. "Have you ever known me to pull any punches when I'm talking to an author?" The woman laughed. "Have I ever once told someone they were good, when they sucked the big one?"

"Not that I've ever heard. Just yesterday you made two authors cry when you told them that they needed to go back to school to learn how to write a full sentence or you were done with them. Oh, and she told Todd, a great author until lately, that he needed to go get laid. And take a vacation. Not necessarily in that order."

21

"Thanks, Margie. Get me Shawn on the line, and also... let me think a moment. Oh, what the hell, get Steven too. Tell them I have a winner." She looked at him. "This will be a movie if I don't miss my bet. And when it is, you're never going to have to worry about whether or not someone paid me to read your stuff or not. The entire world will be lining up to read it."

The phone call was put through and she talked to Steven. He didn't have any idea who that might be, but he wanted her to send the manuscript right over. If it was as good as she said it was going to be, then he wanted it.

"I've never steered him wrong before, so he's happy." Xander nodded at Doris, his head spinning too much to really comprehend what was going on. "Now, as I was saying, you will need to get some book signings set up before this book goes to the top of the list. I want you to have at least three lined up by—" Another scream to Margie again. "Get me that list that was given to me yesterday. Mark the ones that are smaller venues for me."

"I did that yesterday. And if you want me to get him in something, why are you going small?" Doris winked at him as she answered Margie. "Oh. I like that. Have him go there, famous by then, and bring in the people. I love it."

"There will be a few that don't care for a big timer there, but they'll be happy with the sales they get from this. You're going to be bringing in the readers in droves. But you won't be just signing. I want—"

"Wait. Just slow down just a minute." She grinned. "I don't want to sound ungrateful, but what are you talking about? A book signing? Other authors? You've not even published it yet and you're talking to Steven, who I don't know, and this other person, Shawn."

"You might not know them, but you have most assuredly heard of them. But as for book signings, you'll need that too. And…damn, I wish you had a pretty wife at your side. She might be able to save you some women throwing themselves at you." He just stared at her. "All right. You wear a pair of nice jeans. A polo too. I don't want you all stuffy looking. And your hair. I love the way you keep running your hands through it. Makes you seem less like a stodgy author and more touchable. But don't let them touch you. That will get you into trouble faster than robbing a bank."

By the time he left the office, it was late, and he still had to have dinner at his parents' home tonight. The check in his pocket from Steven — there was no doubt in his mind who it was now — was like having a splinter under his nail. He pulled it out three times even before they were on the highway to home. He'd just sold his first book to a big-time director. And he had no idea what the fuck the big deal was. It was a book from a man who…well, he wasn't nothing, but he wasn't anything to take a second look at.

Xander just had the driver take him to his parents' home. He wasn't sure how the trip was made — it could have been on the back of a jet for all he knew. The check, the deal, and the promises made to him were enough to make him both giddy and sick at the same time.

Xander was in the living room, alone, when he heard his mom coming in the front door.

"There you are. I've been trying to reach you all day. How did it go?" He asked her what. "Oh, Xander, you were supposed to meet with Penny's teacher today. Did you forget?"

"No. I don't.... It's tomorrow. Not today. The teacher changed it on me, and I had to move things around today to talk— Mom, what do you know about book signings?" She told him not much on the author side, but as a reader, they were a lot of fun. "I have three lined up for next year."

"Well, that's wonderful. Where are they?" He told her he didn't remember. "You should put it on your calendar, the one you share with me. And I didn't think about checking the calendar today. Are you all right, Xander? You look a little manic if you ask me."

"I feel that way too." She asked him if he was staying for dinner. "Yes. I mean, there still is one, correct? I would have thought I was running late."

"No, dinner is a little late. There were a couple of scheduling issues that needed to be fixed. Gabe had to go to the hospital to help them with another death, poor boy. And Caleb had someone in the pack that died. I believe that the two are connected, but I'm not sure yet." She patted him on the cheek. "You're all right then?"

"I am." He laughed and covered his mouth when it did sound manic. "I have some news. Would you like to hear it?"

"Oh yes, but is it the kind that you can share with us all? I'm thinking we might need some good news after today. Poor Mr. Gallop had four grandbabies. He'll be missed." Nodding at her earned him a kiss on the cheek. "You're looking better now. Have you got whatever it is settled in your head?"

"Yes, I think so. It's been a weird day." She patted him again on the cheek and left him standing there.

Just as he was going to have a seat again, his dad came in with a young woman. But almost as soon as the thought of her being young came into his mind, he knew that she was older than all of them. He started forward to greet her when she backed up. The small insect, the scarab, he thought it was called, was right in front of him. Xander looked at his dad for help.

"Son?" He glanced at his dad, then back at the woman. "Xander, this is Addie. Adaline Dyer. Addie, this is my son, Xander. He won't hurt you."

"My lady?" The scarab didn't stand down but seemed as confused as he was. When he looked at him, coming to stand on his outstretched hand, Xander felt like he'd been given something special. Then he looked at the woman. "She's not sure what to do about you. You're nothing that she expected. Do you know what you are to her? Something neither of us thought was possible, you know."

"I don't know what's going on. If you're saying what I think you are, then I smell nothing from her. Actually, you either."

The scarab cursed quietly, then snapped his...pinchers? The scent from the woman hit Xander hard. Her beauty was something that he'd never seen before. Even as he took a step toward her, his mind was telling him to tread carefully, while his body and wolf were telling him to go forth and conquer. He had a feeling that listening to that part of him would get him killed quicker than stepping in front of a bus. Or an entire line of them.

Xander should have known better. Should have taken to heart what his mind was telling him. Almost as soon as he was close enough to touch her, she jerked him around so that his hand was up behind his back, his knees on the floor. This was no way, he thought, that a mate should treat the other, but he kept his mouth shut. There was more to this woman than just mate to mate. She was too old for that.

The blade at his throat had him not even breathing deeply. She, Addie, wasn't happy to find him, he thought jokingly. But when he felt the blood slide smoothly down his throat to his chest, Xander made himself be very still. Things would work out, he thought, or he'd be dead. But he had a feeling that the woman he was feeling at his back now was more of the way she was all the time than the beauty that his dad thought he knew. A scary hard ass that would rather kill him than deal with his shit.

Chapter 2

Addie paced the spacious room after letting the big man go. She didn't know what was happening...well she did know, but didn't want to believe it. Mr. Winchester had left them in the room alone when she released Xander. He wasn't bothering her, and Addie thought that was what was pissing her off the most.

"You want to have a seat?"

She demanded to know what he meant. Her face heated up when he merely pointed to the couch. "I don't want you to get any ideas in your head. I've enough shit going on as it is. And having you order me around will not settle well with me, so just don't fucking do it."

"I haven't any idea what you mean by ideas or ordering you around. But I have a great many of them—ideas, I mean—circling around all the time now. If you'd have a seat, we can have a calm conversation. I'd like that, even if you wouldn't." She sat, but she wasn't going to talk to him. "First of all, I'm going to tell you something. When I was seventeen, my mate was killed in a grocery store, along with her mom and a dozen or so other people. Finding you now has me...well, I have no idea what I am right now. Confused? Yes. Happy? Oh yes. Calm? More than you are, but I can understand that too. This isn't something that, as you know, happens. A second chance at a mate."

Whatever she had expected him to say, that wasn't it. "I'm sorry." He nodded and leaned back on the couch. "This doesn't buy you any points with me. I'm not going to be at your beck and call either. You have to know right up front, I'm not a pushover."

"Believe it or not, I got that right away. I think it was when you took me to the floor without any kind of explanation. Or maybe when you cut my throat. Either is very telling." She didn't like him. And she was sure that he knew it. "Back to my mate. When she was killed, I assumed, sadly so, that I'd be alone for the rest of my life. Then Penny, my adopted daughter, came to me, and I've been—well, happy. She's the daughter of the woman who was killed and buried in my basement."

"Recently?" Xander told her that it was several months ago. "It was Boone, wasn't it? He was a real bastard, from what I read. And I think he might be the reason that I'm in so much shit right now."

"No, not him, but someone just as bad. Anyway, I only recently talked Penny into allowing me to have her mom brought from the floor and put into the family cemetery. It's been hard on her, as you can imagine. But, thanks to the innocence of children, she could see and talk to her mom all the time. Which is making the transition easier for her." She nodded, not saying anything to him. "Dad told me that you were a para-canvas. I hate to admit it, but I don't know what that is. Nor what it is that you do."

"Yes, I'm a para-canvas. I have guns, knives, and blades on my body. Cate, the woman who's magical, she can put them on me. It's not really a tattoo, as she can remove them, but they are permanent to my body until then. I can use them too, peel them from my body and use them like anyone would a weapon." He told her that wasn't what he meant by what she did. "Then I don't understand."

"The weapons. Why do you need them? What is it you do? I'm assuming you don't belong to a baking club." She told him that she didn't cook. "Me either. I have someone that does it for us."

"I'm not living with you." Xander told her the cook was for him and Penny. "Oh. I'm sorry. I don't know what's wrong with me. I keep hating everything that comes out of your mouth."

"Oh, I don't think you hate everything that comes out of my mouth." She thanked him. "I'm sure you hate whatever comes out of anyone's mouth that doesn't agree with you. You seem sort of pushy and on edge all the time."

Her temper, usually so slow to burn, ignited just like that. As she reached for him, he turned and shifted into his wolf just as she hit him in the face with her fist. Then she was under him, his great mouth at her throat.

Bug moved, then was off her body. She saw him then, sitting upon the large head of the gray wolf. Addie could feel his disappointment in her. For what, she didn't know, but she was sure that he'd tell her.

"Addie?" Mr. Winchester sat down on the floor next to them as he continued. "Xander would like for me to talk to you. He said to make sure that you understood that he could have bitten you to connect with you, but he's not going to do that. All right?"

"She is agreeable." Addie looked at Bug. He'd never spoken before, and when she asked him about it, through their link he told her. *There was never any necessity for it before. And this, my dear lady, is necessary. You have made your mate upset with you.*

"Xander would like to know if you're going to be this violent all the time." Mr. Winchester laughed, and she glared at him. "Well, darlin', you have to admit, you have been a tad on the violent side. And snappish. My grandsons, when they get like that, I send them to their room for a little rest time. Once they get up—"

Xander must have cut him off, because when he straightened up and smiled at her, she could have sworn his face had pinked up. As he listened to his son, she assumed, Addie thought of her temper and realized that she *had* been a bitch. Not once had anyone here called her on it, and here she was, under her mate.

"You didn't answer the question, Addie." She looked at Bug and answered him for Mr. Winchester.

I'm sorry. Not that I know what's going on, but I'm terribly sorry for the way I've acted. It's not like me. Bug cleared his throat. *Just tell him that, will you? This man is heavy.*

"He is also very naked." When Mr. Winchester left them, laughing hard enough that he had to hold onto the wall

30

a couple of times, she asked Bug why he knew that. "His clothing that he had on is shredded on the floor around us. And since I can talk to you and him, I'm going to tell you what he says now. Mr. Winchester said that he is going to have the others have something to eat. I'll help you. So long as you're not nasty."

Why are you on his side in this? She heard him repeat her question to the big wolf. *Stop telling him private things and make him to get the fuck off me.*

He moved. The wolf, however, was gone, and on her now was the naked Xander. She looked into his eyes and saw there something that she doubted that many saw. Intelligence — yes, and she'd bet a great deal of it. Compassion. Understanding. And she could also see that he had a deep set of morals. Not that she didn't think he would, but it was surprising to see it there.

"Can I talk to you without you trying to hit me?" She nodded. When he leaned up on her, his groin was pressed into her. "I'm sorry about this. But you left me no choice in the matter. When you hit me, expect me to protect myself. It's not possible that you could have killed me, I know that, but I was trying to be on my best behavior and you were not."

"I shouldn't have done that. Any of the things I've done since finding you. I told you, I don't know what it is that makes me want to lash out at you. Or hurt you for that matter." He nodded and shifted again. "You have to stop moving around so much. Please. You're...you're distracting me from thinking."

"Maybe that's what you need to do. Stop thinking." He leaned close, his breath warm against her lips. "The little creature, he's a part of you as well?"

"Yes." It was breathless, so unlike her to feel that way. "Where did he go? He was on your head when the wolf was here."

"He's on my back. And when I say that he's on my back, I mean in my back. I can feel him under my skin."

Xander jumped up so quickly that she hurt for a moment when his knee crushed against her thigh. Xander started screaming about bugs and that he was creeped out. As he danced around the room, trying to get Bug to stop moving over him, he turned his back to her and she could see her little sigil racing against the hands that chased him. Addie also got a good look at Xander's ass and his legs. The man was in shape, she'd have to say that about her mate.

Gabe came in then, as did the rest of the family. There were guns out, blades too. But she couldn't stop laughing. That was until he turned around, naked and hard as stone. Xander reached for the pillow on the couch to cover himself when his mom yelled at him.

"I.... She.... Mom, this isn't what it looks like." Everyone turned to her and she stared back. Addie wasn't sure what she could say to them, because she had no idea what was going on. "She has...had a sigil on her chest—there around her throat, not her chest. I didn't see her chest. Just that she had—"

"Son, you're digging and digging at that hole you've got yourself in, and not filling in the hole all that well." He nodded to his dad. "Just tell us what this sigil did to you. I'm assuming that was what happened after you came from your wolf."

"Yes, yes. I shifted from my wolf and I could feel something on me. I felt something crawling on me." He turned around and she could see Bug on his back, moving up and down his spine as if he were looking for an entrance to an elevator or something. When he stopped, Xander turned again, this time tying a throw around his hips. "He's there. I can feel him moving."

I'm claiming him. Even if you don't right away, I must make sure that we can speak. He has my magic as well. Addie told them what he was doing. *He is a large man, is he not?*

"Yes." She looked at his family when she realized she'd spoken aloud. "He needs to mark him. I'm not sure how. I doubt that he'll have a necklace like I do. But it was a gift, from my creator. And now that I have a mate—an unclaimed mate—she will need to come here to claim him as well. I'm not sure if he'll be marked, but that's how she claimed me. Her name is Cate. I don't know how she'll take me having a mate either. More than likely she'll think that it's funny."

"Wait. I need to see...? You were created?" Xander didn't look to be freaking out. Nor did he seem to be upset. But when he smiled at her with a wink, she felt like he'd hit her, with his entire body. "I think we need to talk. After I get dressed and have some dinner. Then, once we've refortified ourselves, you and I will talk. But no hitting or snapping, if you please. Okay?"

"Yes. No. Yes, I think food would be good. And no, I'll try my best not to hit you again. But I'm not making any promises." She sat up and the wound in her side pulled. He moved toward her slowly and she watched him. He looked like his counterpart. The wolf in him looked as if he were stalking his prey. "What do you think you're going to do?"

Her voice was breathless, like she'd run an entire mile, uphill, in the pouring rain. When he asked her to stand, putting out his hand as he spoke, she took it without any hesitation on her part. He got to his knees and asked her if it was all right if he healed her. Before she could get her mind to tell him no, her mouth just went ahead and agreed with him.

"I'm going to heal you, if you'll allow it. You do know how I do that, correct? I don't want you to be upset at me licking the wound." She looked for help, from anyone, but it was just the two of them in the room again. Bug, she had no idea where he was, but he didn't answer her calls to him either. "It'll connect us. I'm sure you don't really want that, but—"

"We are. Connected, I mean. If not, then Bug wouldn't have been able to come to you." He nodded, then asked about the creature's name. "He's a scarab. He was a gift to me when I was created. That was the first name that popped into my head, and he liked it. I'll tell you about it later."

"Yes, I'd like that." He asked her again if he could heal her. "As I said, we'll be connected, you as my mate. Not mated. While I do wish to mate with you, I won't force you into anything. I think I might live longer if I don't."

"I can't hurt you now. I might...I'm sure that I'll lash out at you, but I will *try* to not do that. There are things you have to be aware of, things that could get you killed." He said he wasn't worried so long as she was in front of him. For some reason, that made her laugh. Something she hadn't done in a long time. "Go ahead."

The bandage was removed, and she felt his warm breath

again. It was too much and not enough. And when his tongue touched her, played with her skin a little too long, she moaned. Then he licked end to end and around the bullet wound that had been stitched up. Looking down at him when he said her name, she saw that he, too, was being marked, but not with a necklace.

~*~

Xander stayed very still. He thought at first it was the little bug, but the more it moved over his skin, the more he realized that it wasn't him. Looking down at this chest when he felt something running down his belly, Xander watched the blood seep from the markings that were drawing on his chest. It was moving along his arm and down to his wrist as he watched.

"Does it hurt?" He looked up at Addie and nodded. "I'm so sorry. I had no idea that this would happen. I thought you'd get a small mark, but not like this. And that she'd come to do it for you, not just leap right on you with it."

"It's all right, I think. To be honest with you, I had no idea that I could tat. When you told me, I meant to say something, but it seems a moot point now." She went down on her knees beside him. The pain was really making itself known to him, but to have his mate watching him, he tried to stiffen his body against it. "I'm going to be all right, aren't I?"

"Yes." She didn't sound any more convinced than he felt. But she did hold his hand, and he thought that might be worth the pain of it all. "You're being marked by my owner, Xander. I didn't know that she'd even be able to do that from a distance. She's been on holiday for a long while and will be gone for a few more years, as far as I know. Well, not on holiday, but resting. Creating beings takes a lot out of someone."

"'Tis not her, my lady, but her magic." They both looked at Bug. "If you remember, she said that you might take a man to your bed, but that he would never see what you truly are. But once you found yourself the other half of you, it would complete you both in ways that the world would never know. He will be your other part."

"Other part of what?" Xander hissed when she wiped at his wounds. She told him again that she was sorry, but he only shook his head. He was as close to screaming as he'd ever been. And when he looked down at himself, he could see that the tattoo—sigil, he supposed—was making something artistic.

At the point where his shoulder connected with his arm were large wings. They encompassed not just his shoulders, but under them as well. There wasn't any color in them, not yet anyway, but the rest of the pattern was starting to make more sense.

There were triangles, ten that he could count, from the bottom of the wings to his wrist. When he turned his arm over, there were two rows of ten there as well, along with a shield.

Xander would bet anything that it was the crest of the maker, the seal of his ownership, so to speak. He stood up to look at his chest in the mirror by the door. Wiping at the blood with a tissue, he realized that it didn't hurt at all anymore. And there wasn't any scabbing either.

Just as he was ready to ask about it, he saw the small design over his heart. It was beautifully done, the wolf. He was surrounded by what Xander knew now was wings, but it wasn't until the creature moved that he realized that they were attached to it. The wolf on him had wings, and she seemed to stare back at him. When he moved in the mirror, he was sure that it was watching him. Reaching out to his own wolf, to see if he could somehow speak to him, he was surprised by the voice that answered him back.

"My lord, my name is Asim, protector and guardian. To you and all mankind." The wolf seemed to leap from his flesh and stood before him. "I am your humble servant, Lord Xander. I have not taken your wolf within you, but have become a part of you that will roam the world with you."

The creature before him shook her fur and the wings curled around her. The wolf was smallish, about the size of a medium sized puppy. He'd bet anything that she could have been much larger, but was taking things slowly, just for him.

She was the same color as his gray wolf, but looked more puppy-like than the vicious canine he thought she might be. Thinking of meeting this thing, this part of him, naked, had him pulling the blanket tighter around him.

Xander's skin moved, and clothing appeared on him. At first he wasn't sure what he was wearing. A cloak, some boots that were hard yet made of leather. The shirt he had on was silk, the material almost like a second skin. And when he ran his fingers over the fine material, he thought of jeans and a T-shirt, things that he preferred. And that was what he was wearing seconds later.

The jeans were worn, like he had had them for months. The socks he had on were dark—not dressy, but of a gray color that he liked. His T-shirt was from his college days, the name of his frat house emblazoned across the front. Xander was almost afraid to check his underwear or even see if he had them on. It was too much.

Sitting down, he looked at Addie. "Asim is old school, so dressed you accordingly until you thought of this." He nodded. "Are you wigging out? Do I need to slap you again?"

"No. I don't think so. But yes, slightly freaking out here. You said old school. Do I even want to know what that means?" She didn't so much as blink at him. "I see. I should know, but you're not sure the time is right for me to know."

"Exactly. Shall we go eat dinner?" He sat there, staring at her hand that had been offered to him. "Xander?"

"She called me Lord Xander." She nodded. "Another thing that might make me wig out, so you're saving it for later?"

"Pretty much." She snapped her fingers at him. "Come on. Your questions are not going to be answered right now, so enjoy your evening with your family. And when we're all done here, I'll explain things to them and you. All right?"

Xander looked at her. She was trying very hard not to tell him something. Opening his mouth to ask her what it was, he decided that he had enough shit going on in his head for the moment, and didn't do anything but take her hand and follow her toward the dining room. Before getting there, however, he stopped and pushed her against the door and kissed her.

Waiting might have been smarter. But then, he wasn't sure what waiting might have gotten him. More tats? More than likely not. More of the magic? Dressing like this was almost too much, but he was dealing well, he thought. But then she opened her mouth under his and he forgot everything but the woman he was holding.

She was warm, warmer than any human he'd ever held like this. Her skin was smooth; her hair, when he let it down, was long and curled at the tip. As he moved his mouth along her chin to her throat, he could taste her, the richness of her skin, the power that emanated from her. More than anything, he wanted to bite her, taste her. The wounds had given him only a hint of what she was, Xander wanted it all. She was his.

Lifting his head just enough to look at her, two things occurred to him at once. Firstly, her eyes were the green of dark old emeralds. Secondly, her skin the healthy brown of someone who worshiped the sun. When she curled her hand in the back of his head, pulling him closer to her, he kissed her again, this time pressing his hard cock deep within the folds of her flesh.

"You're all mine." He didn't care who owned who, he told her. "You're mine, Xander. Now and forever. I won't let you be hurt, I'll never allow anyone to be near you but family, and forevermore, you'll be my mate."

He kissed her again—or perhaps she kissed him. Whoever did the kissing, they were both enjoying it. Melting into it. But when he felt the laughter of his brother before he spoke, he lifted his head from hers and rested his forehead on hers.

I hate to tell you this, but Mom knows that you're pounding your mate. The pictures on the wall in here are shaking. He told Tyler to fuck off. She was pounding him. *Oh well, I doubt that Mom will care what the difference is, but how about you two come and join us for a meal? I don't know about you, but hearing you in there is not easy on me. I doubt that it's easy on anyone within a hundred miles, actually.*

39

We'll be in soon. Addie laughed when he told her what was going on. The pup curled around his legs as Bug moved along her shoulder. "Do we have to feed them? I mean, what do sigils eat?"

"What you're having. Asim will want more meat, as does Bug." She moved from under him and toward the dining room, laughing. "Of course, you could just let her chew on your own flesh. I'm sure she'd like that too."

He was still standing there when he saw his mom. She asked him if he was all right. After shaking his head, he told her that he wasn't really sure if he was ever going to be all right again.

"As it should be when you have a mate. I'm thinking that she's going to set you on your ear, and that household of yours. What does she think of Penny?" He told her that they'd not met as yet. "I'd take care of that first thing when you get to the dining room. I know it won't matter much how she feels about—"

"It'll matter to me." She nodded and patted him on the cheek. "Mom, what if she and Penny hate each other? What if they never get along?"

Laughter came from the big dining room—a room, like most homes, he supposed, where families met and enjoyed each other. At least his did. When they were all able to get together, they did have fun. Mostly poking at each other, but he loved everyone at that table whether or not they were blood to him.

When he went into the room, he supposed the idea of introducing his daughter to his mate was a moot point. They seemed to be getting along just fine. Addie was showing

Penny how to eat a steak. Not that it was difficult, but to cut the meat up for a kid might have been something that she'd not done. He knew that in the time Penny had been with him, they'd not had any kind of steaks, so he decided that he needed to broaden her tastes. Expand her menu.

"Oh yeah, I almost forgot to tell you guys." Owen stood up and gently touched his spoon to the glass he was holding. "I found the little box that Michael told me to look for. It was under the floor of the pool house, along with a trunk the size of a car. And before you ask, yes, we did open it. I handed it over to the police. There were things in it, things that will solve a great many cases involving missing and murdered people. There was the last trunk too, one from Birdie. It was filled with the usual things, mostly art and a few cups and such. We're going to put all of it, I think, up for auction. Clare and I have decided to—"

"Get on with it, Owen. They've been wanting something on this for days now. Just tell them what you found, or I will." He grinned at Clare, who hit him in the arm. "He found diamonds. Three cups of them. And I don't mean like those dinky little ones that you might serve a shot of coffee in, but full-sized, twenty-ounce suckers. And they don't belong to anything that we can find."

"Diamonds? What the hell?" Xander's mom hit him in the back of the head as she handed him the potatoes. "Sorry, Mom. But that's a lot of money. What are the plans for it?"

Penny giggled when Owen looked at her. When she stood up, showing off the pretty bracelet that she had on her wrist, Xander glanced at him.

"Every child born to this family will have something made

41

for them that holds the diamonds, so long as the diamonds last. There are a dozen diamonds on the bracelet, which can be used for one thing and one thing only. Education." Owen kissed the back of Clare's hand as he continued. "The boys will also have their diamonds, but we're still working out the details on what they will be made in to. So far, we're talking to someone about having a male version of this made for them."

Caleb said that he was open to ideas if anyone had them, but as far as he was concerned, this was the nicest gift that he could think of to give someone. And that he was upset that he'd not thought of it. "I never have any good ideas." They all laughed. "Seriously. I'm really good at telling someone that was a good idea, but I never have any. I don't think I ever did."

"You used to before you became stodgy." He asked his dad what that meant. "You know, uppity. You're uppity, Caleb."

"I most certainly am not. Why would you say such a thing?" They were all laughing when Dad said he was joking. "Well, it's true. My ideas aren't there for me. Just the kind that I can put to paper."

When dinner was over, and the kitchen was cleaned up, Xander and his new family headed home. His car wasn't at his parents' house, but that didn't bother him much. It wasn't quite cold enough yet that they couldn't walk. As they were going home, Penny asked about the puppy that was running alongside her.

"Asim's part of what I've become." She paused in throwing a stick, and Asim sat down to wait. "She's mine to use when there is trouble. I'll know more later, after Addie and I talk. But if you ever need her, I'm betting that she'll be right there for you."

"Will you be talking about me?" He shook his head, but was cut off from telling Penny the reason they wouldn't when Addie left him to walk with Penny. "I don't want to leave here. I love the house and you guys. My mom is going to come out tomorrow, and I won't know what to do. She told me that she was moving on, but I know I'm going to miss her. Do you think it would be all right if Azim hangs out with me for a little while?"

"As she should. And yes. There is no reason for Asim to be on her master's body. But you should remember not to detain her if she needs to go to Xander. It might get him hurt should you do that." Penny told Addie that's she'd never do that. "Good. Also, you know why your mother has to move on, don't you, Penny? From what I've heard, it's very taxing to be around as a ghost. And your mom, she has to worry about what's going to happen to you, correct?"

"Yes. She said that she loves that Xander took me in and that he's allowed me to be a little girl. I had to have her tell me what she meant. And she said that I didn't have to steal food or hide in the cabinets when he's around." He told Addie that he'd explain that later. "She said that I was going to be happy, but with her there, I can't be fully. I don't want her to feel bad, so I don't like to be happy with her stuck here."

"You are a good daughter." Penny hugged Addie and thanked her. "You run on ahead. I'm sure you have a lot to tell your mom. And make sure you tell her that I'm coming as well. So, she's not disturbed."

When she ran ahead, with the dog with her, Xander told

her everything that he knew. From how her mom had been killed, and then to adopting her so that she could stay with her mom. But in that, he'd fallen in love with the little girl and thought of her as nothing but his child. As he finished the story, he noticed that the house lights were on and that Penny and Asim were in the yard, playing. And Sharon was on the porch.

"She's moving on so that her daughter can have a better life. Penny doesn't leave here much, does she?" He told her that she went to school and sometimes played with Harley and Conrad. "Yes, I can see her taking the time to be with them both. And the other boys, they have issues as well, don't they?"

"Yes. Their parents abused them, mentally and physically, when they were alive and well after they were both dead. They would hurt them by coming to them in the middle of the night to beg them to kill themselves. Just so they could all be together." She looked at him. "Yes, I know. It's difficult to believe. But that's what happened to them. They're stunted in their growth for love and companionship. However, my dad is working on that with them. They'll be out of their shells by Christmas, he told me."

"Your parents, they're good people." He nodded and told her that he thought so as well. "I have to tell you what we are. When I became, as well as why I'm here. Some of it you'll find hard to believe, but you have to be ready. If what I've learned from your sister that can see ghosts is only half true, then you could be in as much trouble as I am."

"With you, I will be as ready as I can be." She didn't look convinced. "Let's talk. I'm sure that while I won't understand all of it, I'm going to help you as best I can. I can promise you that."

She didn't look convinced. That was all right with him. Xander had had a lot thrown at him today and yesterday, and he was— Shit. He'd forgotten to tell them about his movie deal at dinner.

Chapter 3

Addie wasn't sure where to start. She knew the beginning was a good place, but with this, she wasn't sure that was a good idea. So, she decided to give Xander the highlights and hope she didn't overwhelm him too much.

"I was created by a witch for a queen to help with her failing castle. Once I had secured the castle for her, as my reward, she gave me freedom." He put up his hand. "If you ask questions, it's going to take a lot longer."

"Yes, I'm aware of that. But you can't just say you were created by someone and that you helped a queen with her castle issues, and not think I might want some more details." She growled at him. "Honey, I can do that much better than you ever will."

"What did you want to know now?" She'd thought to hurry through this and hope that he would be too overwhelmed to have much in the way of questions, questions that she wasn't sure he'd want answers to. While she would answer them for him, she was positive that they were only going to make more questions, and that would take forever. "Xander, none of this is important to the story."

"Of course it is. Now, who created you? I got that you were made for battles, but how much did you do? Lead, or did you train the men?" She told him she'd fought the war alone. "I see. And this war. How many men did you take down?"

"Twelve thousand." He nodded, then looked at her hard. "Yes, I said twelve thousand. It wasn't as hard as you'd think. I mean, I have a great deal of magic to help. And then there is Bug."

"He's the one that keeps you informed, he told me." Addie sat down and nodded. "Okay, good. All right. Twelve thousand men?"

"Yes. But as I've said, I have magic. Once they saw me on the great white dragon, most of them started to retreat." He nodded again, and she wanted to tell him to use his words. Perhaps she thought, this was his way of dealing with this. "The dragon was something that I could make with my magic. There were dragons at that time, smaller ones than I could have used, but this one had the right effect. They were all dead within moments of me being called upon. I don't mess around with calling a meeting. I like to ask whatever I'm supposed to, and when I don't get the proper answer, I kill. As simple as that. At least back in those days. Now it takes longer because people need answers before they can make a sound decision. Sometimes that takes too long."

"You did this a lot? For this queen? And then she gave you your freedom. I'm assuming then you went on to help others like her." She shook her head and said that she was dead. "But you helped her."

"She had to forfeit her life because of the way that I was created. It was, at the time, good for her kingdom. And her daughter was as good as the queen was, so it worked out. But the men, other kings, the ones that governed the laws of the times, they didn't care for her." She watched his face when he asked her when this had taken place. "Xander, this isn't a good idea. You're not going to like my answer."

"It's before Christ, isn't it?" She nodded. "A long time too, I'm betting. And you were...no, I don't think I want to know anymore right now. Just...just don't bring up how much older you are than me. So, with your age, is this where you gained magic? All of it?"

"Yes. And thank you." He just nodded, but she could see his mind working out the dates. "You have it too. Magic that is mine. I don't know if you have as much as I do, but you have it. We can both shift now, into any living animal or being. The blades that I have, Cate will know if you have any of them coming to you too. Perhaps she's waiting until you're stronger. Or maybe she thinks that you won't need them. I don't know, actually. There was never a mention of an actual mate, other than someone would complete me someday."

"Like you can be a wolf?" She told him she could. He got up to pace. Addie had noticed that about all the Winchesters. They did that when they needed to work things out. She did as well, but with him it was more of a form of art. Or perhaps— "I could use a run. With you. I would really like to get out into the night and do that."

He tore off his clothing. She started to tell him that he could leave them on and shift, but she thought he was right.

Xander was on overload and needed things to be normal, whatever that meant, for a little while. She hoped that he'd be as accepting when she told him the rest. Or they'd be wolves a lot while he worked it out.

The run was just what she needed too. They didn't do much, just ran together, chasing scents that meant nothing to either of them as pack animals. The deer seemed to ignore them for the most part, unless they startled them out of their way. When they were headed to a large structure, he told her that it was the barn at the very back end of Owen's property. That was when they both smelled the man.

I know this scent. She asked him if it was someone that was friendly. *Not really. He's been trying to get my brother to admit that he's killed off someone in order to be able to sell off all these cups and such. I have to let him know.*

While you do that, I'm going to see if he's still around. The scent smells very fresh. She could feel his hesitation, and waited for him to tell her he'd look for the man. But when all he said to her was to be extra careful, she wondered at how much that had cost him, to allow her to go ahead of him. Wolves were very protective of their mates, all females really. And Xander, all the Winchesters, had been raised by a couple who took pride in the rules that were theirs to use. Sara and Kelley were the best family she'd ever known, and their children, sons, in turn were as well.

The scent was stronger the closer she got to the ladder. When she was ready to climb it as herself, she felt the man rather than saw him. Turning slowly, making herself shrink down to nothing more than an ant, she waited for him to come down the ladder and turn to the opening. Whatever he was doing in here, he smelled of fresh hay, and strongly of garlic.

"I thought you were told to stay away from me and my property." Owen didn't look happy as he appeared in the doorway of the barn. Nor was he alone. Xander as his wolf was there beside him. Owen was not at all like the man she'd met only the night before. He was hard, his anger a part of him that she doubted many had seen. "I've called the police. If you leave, they'll just follow you and bring you to justice."

"I'm not doing anything that a good reporter wouldn't do. And since you've had me fired from my job, I've had to resort to doing things that are less than natural to me. Like entering an empty barn. What is it you're doing out here, Owen? Is his body around here? Have you buried him someplace that I'll find? I will, you know. Whoever you're robbing to make all this money, I'm going to figure it out. Today." The man pulled out a gun, and she warned Xander to stay back, that he could and would get hurt. "Now, you're going to tell me where you're getting these things, or I'm going to write an article that will have you all in jail."

"What the hell are you going to do with that? Who do you think they're going to believe? Me? A man that works and lives in this town? Or an unemployed reporter that has been told to stay away from my family? I'm thinking that they'll never believe you again, even if you smack them in the face with the truth. Why don't you drop the gun? You don't want to do this." He said that he really did. "No, you don't. Put the gun away, or so help me, I'll—"

Addie shifted as soon as she saw the finger tighten on the trigger of the handgun. When she took the man to the floor she knew that one shot had fired, but at what, she didn't

51

know. The man beneath her was dead; she simply broke his neck to check on Xander and Owen.

"He shot him." She moved toward the fallen man and put her hand over the chest wound of Owen. "He fucking shot my brother."

Xander was losing his shit, and she had to do something now. "Shut up." Addie heard his teeth snap shut. "Now, you're going to save his life. Just do what I tell you to do. All right?"

Xander calmed considerably when she spoke to him. She could almost see him thinking now, his mind working through what had just happened. But having something to focus on, someone to tell him what to do, was what he needed. Letting out a breath, he calmly spoke to her.

"Yes, all right. Can you do it?" She said that she couldn't, not right now. "All right, what do I do?"

"Put both your hands on his chest and call to Asim. When you feel her, she'll do most of the work, but she's going to take from both of us. You're the stronger of us right now, because I had to shift. Just let her do the work."

She knew the moment that Asim was starting to help. Felt her own sigil move as well to add to their strength. Addie could have saved him without any issues. But Owen would be hers. And right now, with the way things were in a wolf family, it would be safer for her if he belonged to his brother and not another woman. Wolves were highly possessive.

The barn was filled with people. Family had shown up almost as if they'd been ready to be there. When Owen coughed up some blood, they feared the worst. Addie explained that he had to cough out the bullet or he would have it forever.

Seconds later, the bullet, wrapped in a clot of blood, spilled out of his mouth.

"They'll both need juice." Xander sat back on his ass as he watched his brother. Owen was pale but breathing on his own. She handed him an orange and told him to eat it slowly, as he would still cough up more blood to rid his body of the residue. "You'll need to rest for an hour or so before you shift. And when you do, make sure that you have someone with you. You won't die now, but you'll be weaker than you've ever been."

"You saved my life." She said that Xander had. Owen looked at Xander. "I don't know how you did it, little brother, but I can't ever thank you enough."

"Wait. I thought he was an immortal." She looked at Xander when Dominic spoke. "I thought that he couldn't die."

"The bullet was in his heart. That man hit him in the heart when he fired." Xander looked at her then as he continued. "I could feel it; his heart was dying, and he was going to bleed out. When I touched Owen over the bullet hole, it was like I was a part of him. We.... In another minute, he would have been dead."

"Yes, he would have. But he's not, and that's what we have to focus on." They could hear the sirens coming. "If I were you, I'd just lay there for a bit longer. The weaker you appear, the less likely that I'll end up shot as well."

The police came into the barn with guns drawn and their hearts racing. The Winchesters seemed to be friends with all of them, and had them calmed in no time. The man was thought to have fallen down the ladder when he came down to confront Owen with a gun, and she let them think that. It wasn't until later that she figured out what had happened.

"Hello, my lady." The old vampire, Carmen, bowed before her. "It's been a very long time, hasn't it? I wondered what had ever happened to you."

"And I you, my lady Carmen." Carmen hugged her to her and whispered that she was glad to have helped. Addie had wondered where the magic, just a little, had come from to confuse the police officers. "Thank you for that. I take it you have a relationship with them?"

"Oh yes." She pulled away as she continued. "They are my dearest friends. And I have given them immortality, but with a shot to the heart, it does not keep them from dying. You have given Owen and your mate more. I would suggest that you touch them all in the same way."

"What way you are talking about?" She looked at Kelley Winchester as he wiped the huge red and white hankie across his nose. "You saved my boy there by being around. I don't know rightly what you did, but I sure would like for you to give it to all of us if it means we don't have to hurt like that. I think that there is a difference, ain't they? About the immorality that we got from our good friend Carmen and you. Right?"

"There is. I had Xander save his brother so that, if you wish it, I could do the same for the rest of you. No bullet will penetrate your chest, no blade will cut your throat, and you'll live well beyond any being ever born. You're willing to do that?" He nodded and blew his nose when tears started to fall again. "Kelley, you're a good man."

"I'm a daddy that has seen enough of my boys and their mates hurting. You make it so they won't die and I'll do whatever you want. Anything." She nodded. "Anything, you hear me, I'll give you nearly anything that I own, just so's I don't have to feel so helpless when they're 'a laying before me dying like that again. It hurts me; to the core of my beating heart, it surely does hurt me."

"I want you to love me like you do the rest of them." He looked confused and she shook her head. "Or not. Either way, I'll do—"

"Honey, I done already do love you as much as the rest of them. Since the moment you became my son's mate, then you became our daughter too. You don't have to worry none about that." He hugged her tightly and then stood back. "You don't make it easy, I have to tell you, to show you how much we all love you, but we do. Sure as shooting, I do love you. Even before you saved my boy there, I took you into my heart and let you take up a part of it." Then he hugged her again.

It touched her all the way to her core, and she didn't know what to say. No one, not one person but Xander, had ever accepted her like that before. And now his entire family had. Touching each of them gently on the heart, she even gave a little of the magic to Carmen. The woman was her friend too, and deserved to be around for them even in the daylight hours.

~*~

Agent Jamie Riddell wasn't sure what was going on, but she had to talk to Addie, and soon, about what was going on here at the office. The woman had been her mentor, her friend, as well as someone that she could trust. This place was now overrun by big-headed men who were saying that Addie had killed without cause.

"Miss Riddell, we're—" She corrected him again on her being an agent. "Yes, well, for right now you are. We're trying to conduct an interview on what you know of Adaline Dyer."

"I'm not sure that I know any more than you do, Mr. Bird." He told her it was Finch. "Oh yes, you did say that, didn't you? But as an agent for the FBI, I would imagine that you'd know more about her than I would."

"Where would she be right now?" Jamie asked him what he meant. "She's killed over a dozen of my men, is out there doing who knows what to someone else, and I need to find her." His fist slammed down on the table and she jumped.

"You should get your story straight, sir. I heard that it was only seven, not over a dozen. And that someone who had been hiding out in the building where she shot and killed Mr. Boone shot at her. Wounded her in the chest, from what I heard. Then he fell to his death when she returned fire—and yes, she was returning fire, not shooting first." He told her that she knew a lot for someone that didn't know the woman all that well. "First, I never said that I didn't know her. I told you I didn't know where she was. Every time you asked me. As for the details of what I know or don't know, you yourself handed us all memos on why we should be looking for her. There was a breakdown in communication, you said. She wasn't to kill Boone, your men were. If that's so, then why are you saying that she murdered your men when she was following orders that you gave her?"

He slammed his hands down again, but this time she didn't jump. The little device stuck on her blouse was recording everything that was going on. Hers and Addie's boss, Agent Conair, had given them each one the day that this shit went down with the Feds. The CIA being hired by the FBI to do a job. He'd been right, and now he was dead, as well as two people that they had worked with. Jamie figured that the only reason she was alive still was that she'd been out of the country when the shooting had occurred, and had only just gotten back yesterday. Today, she was being "interviewed" by someone in the Feds' office for misconduct on Addie's part.

"Is that what you were told?" She didn't like the way he was asking her. As if she'd just given him a large candy bar and that he wanted more. "Were you told that she was to kill this Boone person? That she was to do it for the FBI?"

She had to think where she'd heard it besides from Conair. When she remembered, the door to the little room was opened and she saw the young man that had arrived with Finch earlier this morning. His whisper was just loud enough that she heard him.

"Her place is tagged. And so is her phone now. There isn't any way that she'll be able to call or talk to anyone without us knowing. Also, there's a device on her car. If she gets out of hand, we'll just cut her brake lines like we did the other guy." Jamie looked around the room, wondering again what the fuck was going on. "You want us to shadow her too?"

"Yes, yes, that'll be good." He turned back to her. Finch looked so self-satisfied that she wanted to slug him. Instead, she asked him if everything was all right. "Yes, why wouldn't it be? We're the FBI, missy—we are always in the right. Now, what can you tell me about Adaline Dyer? You give me everything and I'll decide what it is that I know and don't know."

It was on the tip of her tongue to point out that she was

57

with the Central Intelligence Agency, but she didn't. Thinking ahead, she decided that she was going to find Addie, by whatever means possible, and let her know, somehow, what was going on here, and how much trouble she was in.

The talking went on for hours. She was much better at the round house than he was. He'd ask her a question, she'd turn it around until he wasn't sure who had asked. Jamie also kept at him with his grammar. When he mispronounced a word, she told him. Used the wrong verbiage, that too was pointed out, until she had him so flustered that he didn't know what way was up.

"Miss...I guess I should continue to call you Agent—for now at least, as I said. Agent Riddell, I'd like you not to discuss what has been talked about in here. Also, and you had better be aware of this, this is an ongoing investigation and you had better play ball with us. When you hear from Dyer, you're to tell me. If she sends you a fucking letter or post card, I want it. You're to tell me whenever you have any contact at all with her. Do I make myself clear?"

"Yes, of course. Very clear." She stood up and he did too. "You have a nice day, Mr. Bird. And don't forget that I work for the CIA, and I only report to one person. And since he's not said a word to me, I will not be reporting anything to you. But you go on thinking that you have some sort of control over me and what I do all day long."

She was shaking when she left the little office. Anger did that to her. And when she was this upset, she cried. Not because she was upset, but simply because she didn't know what to do with such anger.

Jamie knew that she'd made an enemy in the man, and

that was scary enough. But she had to go about her day and make plans. Whatever they were doing, Jamie was positive that she was going to be the next person to have a pretty little headstone.

First things first. She had to contact her leap leader and dad. Columbus had a large cat population, and her dad was leader of them. Being a cat, a tiger, she knew that he would be the only reasonable person that could and would keep her alive. Being in Washington so much, it was difficult to have much in the way of cat time. But she had managed so far. As soon as she sat down at her desk, he told her that he was too busy to talk to her today.

I'm in deep trouble, Dad. He chuckled, and she asked him what was so funny. *I'm serious, Dad. They're looking for Addie, and I could be next.*

His voice changed then; he was all serious for her. *Tell me what you need, baby girl, and you'll have it. If it's about work, over those other deaths, I'll come for you myself.* She told him that would be good. *We'll have some dinner, you and I, and when we're all done, you'll disappear like a fart in the wind. All right?*

Honestly, she was afraid that what he was saying was true—that she would disappear. But would she be alive, that was the question. Jamie hated to make a mistake like this, but her dad, for all his faults, would keep her alive.

Yes, but less like a fart and more like a cat. These men mean business. They've tapped my phone and my apartment. Also, there is a bug and a tracker on my car. I don't want to drag you into this any more than you already are, but I'm not sure where to go. They're looking for Addie. To blame her for the death of that Boone man. He asked her what she had. *You've always been too smart*

59

for your own good. I have things that will make it so she's not guilty on this. Not a lot, but some.

Jamie had a great many things, but she didn't want her dad to know. Not yet. She had Addie's contract with the Feds, the canceled check from the pay off, as well as all the notes that Conair had taken when he was in the meeting. And a recording of the one she just had with the Birdman.

Damn girl. I would say that you're paranoid, but I don't think you are. I'm calling you right now. We'll make plans over the phone for them. You be all gushy toward me, and I'll let you pick up the tab.

She was still grinning when she picked up the ringing phone. After making the arrangements for him to come into town and have dinner with her, she set to work at her desk. She didn't use this computer for anything. Not things like looking for information that wasn't on the up and up. But she did pull out things from her desk and drop them into her purse. She wasn't worried about them finding the things she had taken. Jamie had a little special bag that a faerie had given her when she'd been a child that she could hide a body in should she need to. And if things got as bad as she thought they might, she might have her dad hide her in it to get away.

At the end of the day she was no less stressed than she had been before. Nor any closer to finding the man who was looking for Addie. She could contact her, but not from anywhere around here. She had to get in touch with her friend and sigil. That was the only way.

The wand was used over her person on her way out. Jamie knew the drill. Her purse was open to the man standing there, and when Finch joined him, she made sure that she turned so that whatever he did to her things would be recorded. Watching him as he picked up her bag, she smiled at him when he dumped it out.

"We can't have things going out of here that don't belong to you, now can we?"

When he reached for her little box that held her tampons, his hand was suddenly grabbed from behind. Jamie looked up at the man standing there, her boss's boss, the president of the United States.

"President Baker. I had no idea you were in town." He took the little case from Finch and put it with her other things. "We've had some reports that files are leaving this office."

"And that concerns you how, Finch? Last I knew, your office wasn't even in this building. Why don't you go there and figure out what to tell me when I visit you? But first, you're going to apologize to Agent Riddell here for going through her personal items. That is something that also doesn't concern you. And you were rude. I do not stand for rudeness." She started to pick her things up. "No, he's going to do it. And do so neatly."

She wondered if he had any idea how difficult he was making this on her. But when he winked at her, she was sure that he did and simply didn't care. As she was waiting on her purse, she told her dad what was going on.

Yes, I talked to him earlier. He's a good guy, and he's joining us for dinner. Don't worry about being tagged or whatever they call it. Ben and I have it all taken care of. She asked him if he was going to take care of her when she lost her job. *You know that I will, but you've nothing to worry about. I've got your back on this.*

She hoped so, because the looks she was getting from

Birdman were enough to make her think that he wanted her dead ten minutes ago. When she was handed her purse, she felt the small stab in her finger and jerked back. In that moment, she was terrified he'd poisoned her. But the president grabbed his hand and held it above his head while he hit Birdman square in the face. Christ, this was getting completely out of hand.

While he was laying there, unconscious, she held her finger to her mouth. No one was getting her blood. Not unless she allowed it. The president looked at her and then at the door. Her father was coming through it like he owned the building. Before he could get within ten feet of Birdman, the guards stopped him.

"I have it, James. Let these gentlemen handle it for us." Dad nodded, and she went to him. She was in more serious trouble than before. Now she was dead if she didn't get someone to help her. "All right then, let's go and have a nice dinner."

She was hustled into the limo. Just before getting in, her purse was taken from her and put in another car. As it sped off, she looked at President Baker. He smiled at her and asked if she'd sit up. The wand over her person this time went off a great deal. She was told that she'd have to strip down as soon as they were safe. Safe to her meant home. But that wasn't going to do the trick this time. She knew it too. To these men, it meant being flown to the White House.

Her first visit, and she was being handed a robe and a metal case. As soon as she stripped down, another woman came in and cut several tags, chips, from her body. This was going badly, she thought. Bad as fuck. She only hoped that

Addie was having a better time at this. But mostly that she was alive.

Calling to Bug, she asked him to come to her, now. She was in deep trouble, and so might Addie be. The code they had was to give numbers, not names or places. Jamie hoped that she'd be able to save her.

Chapter 4

Addie looked over the note of numbers that had been given to Bug. There was something about them that she should know, but whatever they were, she didn't know at the moment. Something made her want to run right out and find a secure line, but she wasn't stupid enough to jump to any kind of conclusions. Not at her age. Besides, she didn't think it was a phone number.

She looked over at Xander when he sat beside her on the couch. The run had done them both a world of good. But now they had to talk. And she was sure that she wasn't going to be able to fob him off this time.

"Okay, you know what I want to hear. Right?" She nodded. "All right then. We've killed a man between us, saved my brother's life too. Given enough of ourselves to keep my family alive, a vampire can now be in the sun all day, and we've not had sex. Not once. I'd like to remedy that right now. Or talk. Talking has it points too, but I need you."

"I don't understand." He made a circle with one hand, thumb to finger, and stuck his other finger through it in a fucking motion. "I know what sex is, you idiot. What I don't understand is why you don't have any questions for me."

"Oh, I have lots of those. More than I think I've ever had before. But I need you in the worst kind of way, and you and I are going to bond and mate. I can't stand not having you as a permanent part of my life." He pulled her to him, over him, so that she was straddling his legs. "Kiss me, Addie. Make me your mate so that I can be one with you."

She did kiss him, giving him all that she could in it. And when he pushed her away, it was all she could do not to smack him in the face and take that grin off of it. But all he did was stand her on her feet and pull her to him. Addie cried out when he jerked her clothing off her and buried his mouth over her pussy.

"Yes, that's it. Please, yes."

Xander ate her like she was his first meal. His wolf's touch, the feel of him there, made her come hard. When he pulled back again, she told him to finish her, and all he did was tell her it was his turn.

"I need to come or I'm going to hurt you. And the way I feel right now, you might not get enough from me if I take you on this couch." Her mind was fuddled, her heart racing. "Addie, suck my cock."

Gladly, her mind screamed at her. Dropping to her knees, she did the same as he'd done—ripped his clothing off his body and took him into her mouth, all in one swift movement.

Xander cried out, but he didn't give her what she wanted. His body was hers, she'd told him that before. As she took him deeper into her throat, cupping his hot full balls, she thought of what it would be like to have him inside her, his body filling her in a way that she knew no one else had or ever would again. As he held her head to him, she sent him thoughts of her being eaten, of him fucking her bent over the back of the couch, a chair, anything hard enough to hold her and his taking. And when her mouth filled with him, she swallowed him down so as not to miss a single drop of him.

They had no need for words now. Xander wasn't any gentler in his touching her than she was being. Her breasts were bruised by his mouth and hands as he shoved her to the floor. Her back landed on something hard, but she didn't care. The small device, it looked to be a remote, was tossed across the room when he found it.

Xander filled her, his cock tearing her apart with not just his size but his length too. Wrapping her ankles around him, she was rewarded with more of him, his cock feeling like it was at the back of her throat, it was so long and thick.

She bit at his skin, his muscles, anything that she could touch. He did the same, his wolf too when he was freed enough to mark her. And when he threw back his head, his wolf running along his skin as he howled, Addie joined him. With each splash of his cum, she came. It was the best ride she'd had in her life, and he was giving it to her. When he fell atop her, his teeth sinking deeply into her shoulder hard enough to break bones, she did the same to him, marking her mate for all time.

They dozed off, and when he woke her by crying out again, she thought that she'd hurt him. But the blood smearing over their bodies made her realized that he was being marked yet again, her body as well. As soon as he passed out from pain or the magic that was doing it, she picked him up and took them both to the bedroom she'd slept in alone for the last two nights.

"What's happening?" She watched the hieroglyphics as they formed over his body. "Addie, what's going on?"

"Your story is being marked on you." He didn't know what that meant, but it didn't matter. He passed out again as his entire life was inked over his legs and arms. Addie read them, each line of his life, each mark that was put upon him. And when the one that created her, the witch, Cate showed herself, Addie asked her why.

"He is your other half, my lady. And a king in his own right." Addie didn't understand and told her that. "All that you inherited, the kingdom as well as the riches, they are yours and his now. You will run the kingdom as you should have long ago."

"I told you then that I had no use for a kingdom. I only want to enjoy life." She asked if she had until now. "It matters little now, does it? You've marked him."

"Nay, my lady, you have marked him by taking him to your body. You were told this would be your fate, that someday a man would come to you. He would love you like no one else would. Care for you when others would wish you dead. And that someday, you'd have him a child, a daughter, just as the two of you are." The witch looked at Xander as he stared at her. "You are a good man, Xander Alton Winchester. A better man than I could have hoped for in someone to care for Adaline. The child that you have, sadly, will be the only one sired by you and of her body. But you will have more

68

come into your lives should you wish it. Not all shifters, but some."

"What have I become?" Addie started to answer Xander, but he spoke again. "You've done something to me. This marking that I now have, you've given me magic that I might not want."

"You will not only want it, young lord, but you will need it in the coming years. The decades will not be easy for you both, but you will have each other, and that will bring you out on top of it all. And you will have riches, not just in coin and pretties, but riches of friendship, family, and loyalty." He said that he was rich enough. "Yes, you are. You all are. But you will have a large family, and it will help with their lives as well."

Addie crawled into bed with Xander. He held her as the witch—her name was never known to him, but he thought her to be Cate—helped him to understand what was going on. That no one would see the marks on them unless they needed to, and that need would be from anyone that would call out to have help from the new lord and lady of the castle.

After the witch left, they laid there for a while. The room was dark now, and the moon was streaming through the open curtain as Xander rubbed his fingers up and down her back. It was both soothing and relaxing to have him be with her and to touch her so gently.

"I don't usually have such violent sex." She looked down at him. "I'm sorry if.... You know what? No, I'm not sorry. It was fucking fantastic. And I think you enjoyed it as well."

"Yes, I did. But that's not to say I'd not like gentler sex too." He pulled her to him for a kiss, one that was more like him, she thought. Gentle and loving. "You're the best thing that has ever happened to me."

"You too, love. And I do love you." The note was still burning in her mind, and she wasn't sure what to do about it. "You want to tell me what has you suddenly tense? Or I can just ask you about the note you got today."

She looked at him. "Who...? Asim told you." He told her that she'd been worried about it. "Yes, as am I. I don't know the number. I thought it was a phone number, but now I'm not so sure."

"Let me have a look at it. I might see something that you don't." She got up and handed the note to him that she'd left in the living room. "I'm not even going to ask you how you did that. I'm assuming that I can do that as well?"

Nodding, she handed him the note and waited while he looked it over. When he sat up, she did as well and asked him what he'd seen. This was good, she thought, having an extra set of eyes in this.

"It's not a phone number but a location. Longitude and latitude. I can look this up in no time. Let me see." He was dressing himself with magic as he made his way to the closet. Xander turned to look at her as he stood there. Opening and closing his mouth several times, he just left her there on the bed. Following him, dressing as well and laughing at him, she was entering the office he'd been using as Grayson, the man they had hired to cook for them, entered with a tray of food and drinks.

"I heard the two of you coming down, my lord. I thought you could use something to eat, as you missed dinner." She thanked him and told him they were fine now. "My lady, your...the creatures are awaiting word from you that they may eat what I have set out for them. Red meat mostly, with a bit of chicken for flavor."

"I'll let them know that they may eat, Grayson. Thank you for thinking of them." He hesitated again, and she sat down. "What is it? Something I can help you with?"

"Yes, my lady. Young Penny needs someone to sign a permission slip for her to be allowed to go on an outing at school. I have assured her that either of your signatures would be fine, but she worries so, with her mother coming out this afternoon."

"I'll take care of it for her. And when she wakes, let me know. I'll have a talk with her. I don't blame her for being a little unsure. I am as well." Xander said that he had it, and asked Grayson to have his parents come to the house. He told him the time. "Oh, well, when it's a little later, or earlier, however you want to think about it, that'll be fine with me."

She sat with Xander when Grayson left to get the permission slip. "So, where is this place? Am I going to be upset when you tell me?" He said he didn't honestly know. "Where are we going then?"

"Washington DC. Do you know anyone there? I mean, besides your office and the Feds, who are trying to kill you off. Why would someone send you this without any kind of information?" She had a sudden thought. "Who? Someone that could be in trouble?"

"Yes. Her name is Jamie Riddell. She and I were agents. However, she was the computer one, I was the hit man. Her intel would get me close enough to whoever and I'd take them out. Without her help, Bug and I would have been going in blind to most situations." She asked him where this location was. "It might be her dad. He's the leap leader of the tigers there. But I'm not sure why she'd send this and not just tell me to come and get her."

"I don't know either. But I have to be here today. I could reschedule, but I don't think that would be fair to Penny. Do you need to go now?" She nodded. "I wish you had a better answer, love."

"I have to figure this out. If you were free or even better with your magic, then I'd say reschedule. But if this is Jamie, or her father, then they need me now." He told her to go now then. "Are you sure? I hate to leave you after we're just getting to know each other."

"You go. Now. Because the sooner that you get there and fix this, the sooner you can return. Just promise me that you'll be safe. I can't stand the thought of losing you to someone." Addie promised him that she'd be all right. "I know you will. But that doesn't mean that I won't worry. Perhaps I can get Charles to come here and see about writing the second book. Christ. I sold the book to be made into a movie." He looked up at the ceiling and then at her. "I think the check they gave me is toast."

"I'll fix it for you." She was still laughing when she disappeared after giving him a kiss. "Behave while I'm away. And think of ways to be romantic. I might need it when I get back. And you can call me through our link but not on the phone—not that I have one, but you can contact me. All of you can."

She hoped that everything was all right and that Jamie and her father just wanted her to visit. But she knew better.

72

Even though Jamie had been on vacation while this all went down, there were people around that wanted her dead and would stop at nothing to get her. For whatever reason.

Instead of going right to the location, she made herself small again and went to the place quietly. As soon as she entered the large storage area, she was sure she wasn't going to be able to come back right away. There were lions and tigers everywhere she looked, and none of them looked to be friendly.

~*~

Lyman Finch didn't like the way things were going. First of all, what the fuck did the president have to do with any of this? Of course, he did report to him, or was supposed to, but how did he get to the offices so quickly? And why was he there just when he was going to plant something on Riddell?

"You do know that this puts a damper on things for us, don't you? I mean, if she knows anything, we're not going to be able to get it from her with her under the watchful eye of the president." Lyman wanted to slap the piss out of his brother and partner, Leo. "All you had to do was kill one woman. One, Lyman, and now we're being watched. How the hell do you manage to fuck things up all the time?"

He'd not wanted Leo as a partner. He didn't even want him as a brother. Long ago, Leo had been crippled, and since then he'd been playing it up to the point where Lyman wished him dead. Not aloud, but he would go to bed at night wondering why the gods would not have taken him out of the picture instead of letting him torment him.

"I don't fuck things up all the time. I have trouble with executing everything that we're doing while you sit there and be yourself. Besides, I still don't understand why I have to be the one to do this. Why don't you hire someone to kill her off? I mean, I have my reasons for wanting her dead as well, but fuck this shit." The wheelchair that his brother Leo was in whined when he moved. He hated that sound more than he did his brother's voice. The thing had cost more than his car did, so he was sure that Leo had put the whine in it to get on his last fucking nerve. "Don't come any closer. I told you that you smell. Don't you have someone that can bath that stench off you?"

The wooden spoon hit him right between the eyes. Lyman saw stars for a moment, and when he felt the sting of it a second, then a third time, he grabbed out for it and knocked his brother onto the floor and out of his wheelchair. Lyman went flying off his own chair because of it.

Fuck this shit, he thought as he pounced on Leo and tried to pull him to where he could get a better grip on his throat. But the belt that was forever in his father's hand hit him twice before he was able to get out of the way of it. Fucking bastards, both of them.

"What have I told you over and over about beating your brother? He's in a wheelchair, Lyman. Not some kind of punching bag for when you feel down in the dumps." He pointed out that he'd hit him first. "And how do you think he did that? And why must I point out to you, daily — heck fire, hourly — that he's in a wheelchair? You should be cutting him some slack."

"Father, he's not as saintly as you seem to think he is." Father; he wasn't Dad. they'd stopped calling him that when they were children. "Father, why do you always assume that he's this nice person? Can you see the bump on my head where he hit me? Besides, I have to go to work tomorrow and explain to them why I'm hurt."

"Yes, well, I'm sure that you'll come up with a good lie. You seemed to have a lot of practice at it." He was a grown man, and his father was treating him like he was a four-year-old. "Lyman, what is this I read about you being investigated in the murder of a man by the name of Boone? Isn't he that fellow that killed all those people some time back? I thought you and your brother were working on something about a woman. Like I told you to do."

"Yes. Where did you read that?" Father held up the newspaper rag that was at the end of every grocery store in the world. "None of that is true. I've also told you that nearly all of it is made up and the rest is just lies. As for the woman, yes, that's what pissed...ticked off Leo. Why am I doing this, Father? Why not hire someone to go out and kill that woman? I've done the others for you."

"So you've said to me. But how do you explain that they got your name in here? It's not as if you're all that important to anyone." He pointed out that he was in the FBI. "Yes, so you say. But I have yet to see you on that program. What's the name of that program you and I watch, Leo?"

"*FBI Files*. It's really good show. And they solve these closed cases all the time. And Father is right, you've never been on there. But then, I guess that's all lies too. Right, Agent Lyman?" He could have gladly pulled out his gun and shot the both of them in the head and felt better about life in general. "Let me guess. They don't allow you on there in case someone sees you out and about. They might maul you for your signature. I'm betting the only mauling you get is from some woman that you tried to fuck and disappointed."

"It's autograph, you moronic fuck, and I don't ever disappoint women." He did, but they didn't have to know that. Now it was getting so bad for him that he had to pay for sex. And he hated the way they made him feel, too. "Those are actors, in the event you missed that when they start talking. And while not all of that is lies, they do enhance things to make it more dramatic. Like the pause in the cut away. Surely you don't believe all of that crap, do you?"

Apparently, they did. Lyman had no idea if they were true or not, but he wasn't going to allow his brother to win this argument. It was bad enough that all they did was sit around thinking up ways to humiliate him. But to make fun of his sex life was going too far. That was why he wanted to do this job for his father. Something about her killing his best friend or something. He was never clear on why his father had asked him to do something about her.

Lyman had been so happy that his father had wanted a favor of him, he never thought to question why. Or for that matter, what he had to do. To do a favor for the one man that had respected him less than Lyman did his brother was special. Until he figured out what it was.

He thought about the contract that he'd ordered for Addie to sign off on, the one that wasn't real but a fake one to have her kill someone. For some reason he'd been slightly bothered by the fact that it was perfect. Every sentence had been the same on a real contract taken out, the one that would have her killed. Each line was the same length, and even where the seal had gone, it was there too. Identical in all ways. He didn't know why that bothered him, but it did. Forging the contract that had her working for some left-wing party had been a brilliant idea. She'd gotten a copy of it when asked and he had his. But he'd found all the copies, save one, and he wondered now where it had gone.

Lyman had taken care that all the copies were gone, destroyed, and that the people that had been in the room were dead as well. But he knew, just fucking knew, that that woman, Riddell, knew something he didn't.

Going to his room, he sat on his lumpy bed and thought about it. But he was distracted by the spring pinching him in the ass. Again. Why he'd moved in here was beyond him. Lyman wanted his own home, a new bed, new everything. But there had been trouble abounding when he'd been graduating, and that had followed him into the real world. Even now, people would bring it up.

He'd had to move back home right after graduating from the FBI academy because of a woman. There had been trouble with this woman trying to claim that he'd done something to her and tried to cover it up. He'd not done anything like that, not alone anyway. Smiling to himself, he thought about how hard he'd fought to be found innocent. No one, not any, would believe him, but there wasn't any proof. And since they couldn't prove it, he got to graduate. But they had kept their eye on him since he'd been in the department. In actuality, what had gone down should have been a death warrant to his ability to be an agent.

They said that he and a man that had looked very similar to him had raped a girl in the dorms. She'd been drugged and then raped. But both men, she'd told the police, had worn condoms as well as when they tied her up, they had worn plastic all over their body. Because Leo had been unable to perform such an act—an act, they'd called it—he'd been let out. But, as he knew, there wasn't any DNA to get either of them into court. Lyman had not done it, but the problem was, he could never prove his innocence any more than they could prove that he had done it.

"When are you going to go get us some dinner?" He glared at the door, pulling out his weapon when his father pounded on the door again. "Lyman. Stop jerking off to that catalog and go to get us some dinner. We have decided on that chicken place. We've already written up what we want, so high tail your butt out and pick it up. Now, darn it."

And because he was living here—rent free, his father reminded him all the time—he was the one that was going to run and tote for them. Like he had nothing better to do than to do their errands and run food back and forth. They'd even call him at work and have him pick up groceries on the way home. As if he had no life other than to be there for them. This shit was getting mighty old too.

Getting into his beat-up car, he drove to the chicken place that had just opened. He had a list, as his dad had said, of the things that they wanted, and he simply told the girl to double it and to add some extra mashed potatoes without gravy in it. That was for him. His back had been sore since he'd had to kill Agent Farquhar. And every time he had to sit for very long, it hurt more. Lyman figured he could eat his potatoes lying on his bed. Gravy would just be too messy, he thought.

Killing Farquhar hadn't been easy. He should have thought of how heavy the man was when he decided that in order for it not to look like murder, he had to change up his MO. The man weighed about two hundred pounds, and all of it was muscle.

The killing hadn't been too hard—he'd knocked him down the stairs. But to have to hang him like he had, it had cost him every muscle he had and some he didn't. Christ almighty, what did that guy eat? Cows standing in the field?

He was laughing when she called his name. And when he handed over his credit card, he waited on his receipt. This was a business expense, or it would be when he was finished with it.

As soon as he was in his car and on his way home again, he thought of his family. His mom had disappeared a while back. She'd just left one day after he'd gone to school and not returned—or so his dad had told him. Lyman had thought it was odd that she'd not even taken her car, but Dad explained that she had left it behind in lieu of payment for her half of the household expenses. Like a twenty-year old car would help all that much. But Leo had told him the real story—that their father had murdered their mother and buried her near the house.

If only he could blame this entire mess on both of them, he'd be free of them. But it wasn't going to happen. Not in this lifetime. And all because of one woman—Adaline Dyer. He'd been willing to have her killed by his own men simply to have his father like him. But it had been more than that. Lyman had liked her in the beginning. Now he loathed her as much as his father did.

He'd been asking her out for weeks before all this. Well, he'd been leaving her notes on her desk. Flowers when he could, as well as chocolates. Lyman had tried everything he could think of to get her to go out with him. Then one day, he finally got the balls to approach her.

She'd been talking to her boss, Conair, about some kind of gun that she'd been using. Specs—he knew that was what they were called. He had no idea. Since he'd graduated from the academy, he'd not once looked at another book on guns, knives, or safety equipment. So when she asked him what sort of rifle he used when out in the field, he'd had no answer for the woman.

"Don't you hit the range, Agent Finch? Not at all?" He said that he was busy over at the FBI. He said it so that she'd have no doubt that he was a busy man. "But you have time to stalk me. I want you to stop it, Lyman. You and I, we're never going to happen. I don't date within the job. Hell, I don't date at all. I'm not sure I'd ever date an agent anyway, but not you. All right?"

"That's for sure." The other man, Cody, he sat down with him. All Lyman wanted to do was ask her out, and now he had an audience. "I've been asking her out for months. Gives me this story about how I have a wife and six kids. I only have four."

Agent Cody had no wife, nor did he have children as far as Lyman could find out about him. He did date a great deal, sometimes every night, but no children, and he doubted even now that he'd ever asked the woman out. She wasn't his type. Lyman wasn't even sure she was his type.

Addie and Cody were laughing, and even though he wasn't sure what the joke was about, he laughed as well. When he realized they were not going to leave her alone long enough for him to speak to her, he asked her out on a date. The two men peeled away like they were a skin to her banana.

"I told you, Lyman, I don't date. Thanks though." He nodded, then asked her why not. "Well, first of all, I don't date, as I've said several times. And secondly, I don't care for you. You might be a nice guy and all, but there is something about you that makes me want to run away. I don't know, perhaps it's only me. But no, I'm not going to go out with you. And you should really stop sending me things. Notes and such aren't for the workplace."

"But I want to take you out." He sounded, even to his ears, like a whiney ten-year-old. "Please? We can have a really good time. We'll see a movie and have dinner."

She was shaking her head, and he knew then that she was going to tell her buddies that he was such a baby and couldn't take no for an answer. They'd laugh it up, have a good one on him, and he'd be the laughingstock of the CIA in no time. There was no hope for it. So he had been out to get her long before his father had asked him about killing her. The favor, as he'd deemed it, had gotten him into more shit than the rape of a woman that he'd not touched.

Fuck that shit.

After that, he'd decided that he was going to figure out a way to get back at her. And when his department was in charge of transporting Boone to his home after the interview, his father decided that it was the perfect time for him to get back at them. By killing the woman that had laughed at him behind his back. While he'd never seen her do it, he knew that she was.

Having his brother hack into the system got him all the

information he needed. Leo didn't know why he needed it, other than another lie that he'd told him. And that had made him his partner. In what, Lyman didn't know, but Leo liked the title and that was all it took. Now this shit.

When he got home, they dove into the food like they'd not eaten all day. Which, since he'd not been there to serve them, they might not have. And when they ate every bit of the food, including his potatoes, he wished then that he'd tripled the order.

It was getting harder and harder for him to want to be around these people. Lyman supposed that he really hated all people, and that was why he'd become an agent. His hopes to blow away a few people out of his life, namely his family, and get away with it had failed him as well.

Chapter 5

"Then when we were jumping out of the winder, this here guy came at us with a knife. An Injun. I ain't never seen one of them before. Have you, Xand?" Xander was taking notes today instead of writing. And Charles was proving to be very entertaining. Which was good—his mind was worried about Addie. He told him he'd never seen a real Indian. "Well, I have to tell you. I sure hope to never seen one again. They're a frightful bunch with their long hair hanging down. Did you know that they put grease on it to keep it smooth? Tried that once. All it did was make the dogs follow me around to have a nibble of it. Durned dogs anyways."

Today he was going to take notes, then tomorrow, when Charles had to rest from today, Xander would spend the day writing, transcribing his notes into a spreadsheet then making them into a story. He was also going to be here this morning when the crew came in to look at the subflooring of the basement.

Today was the day. Penny was at school, and he was going to hopefully have her mom out before she returned. Quinn was going to pick her up after school, then take her out with his mom to go shopping for her birthday. It was a big one, he'd been told — she was going to be twelve. Her last year as a little girl. Xander wasn't sure what turning the magical twelve was all about, but he went with it. Like he did a lot of things when it came to girls and such.

He wanted to go and spend the day with Addie. She was gone still, but might be home at any moment. Besides, as she had pointed out, he couldn't help her. Xander was reasonably sure that she didn't want him around because he distracted her. Which he did, as much as he could, he thought with a smile.

"You thinking I might be able to go and see the movie when it's done?" He asked Charles how far he could travel. "Durn near anywhere I wanna go. Last time I was having a hankerin' for a bit of sight seein', I traveled all the way to California." He said the word like it was five syllables instead of four.

"You do realize that things have changed a bit, don't you? I mean, we can travel all the way there in a plane and it only takes a few hours. And travel around the entire world in no time at all. I'm not sure how long, but less time than it did when you were a young man." Charles said his favorite words, *hot dang*. "Yes, well, we can drive there too, but that takes a bit longer."

The doorbell rang, and he told Charles he'd be back. Of course, the ghost went with him. As they were making their way to the front, Asim appeared in front of him. Shaking his big head, he told Xander to move out of the way of the door.

"I don't know who the people are." He asked how many. "Dozen or so. I have sent Bug to check to see—"

The door exploded inward and in walked four men, armed with their guns up and pointed right at Xander. At the order to get to his knees, he did so, but watched Asim. She was growling like she was going to rip their throats out. As he watched, the wolf spread out her wings and grew to about the size of a horse. This was not going to end well for the men. He'd be fine, he knew, but not so much the men.

"Call her off." The man in front screamed at him again and again to call her off. But until he knew what the fuck was going on, he wasn't doing anything of the kind. Then he saw Addie, and she was carrying someone in her arms. Standing, a shot was fired at him just as Asim leapt. He didn't feel anything, so he thought that whatever had been done, he'd not been a victim.

Things were hairy there for a few minutes. It wasn't until a large man in a pair of jeans and a sweatshirt came through the door that it started to calm. He was barking orders like it was his job, and everyone seemed to be following them all.

As soon as Xander touched the woman that Addie was holding, he could feel her exhaustion and fear.

"I've put her to sleep so we could travel here. She's been hiding for the last couple of days. We have to keep her from being found by the Feds." He told her anything that she wanted. "This is my friend, Jamie Riddell, the woman I was telling you about. I'll tell you more as soon as we get her hidden away. Her dad is here too."

He looked at the man still barking orders, and he smiled

at him. There was something familiar about him, but he just couldn't place him. As he and Addie started up the stairs, a cat, a tiger, came with them. He surmised that it was the father, but that didn't explain who the other man was.

Jamie came awake just as the large tiger got up on the bed with her. Almost as soon as she saw him, Jamie hugged the cat to her and sobbed. She wasn't making much sense, but it mattered little, as she was safe while she was here.

"I've brought a team with me to keep us all safe. They're going to your parents now. I'm sorry about the door." He said it was all right and told the man, the stranger, to have a seat. "You have no idea who I am, do you? I'm sorry about that. I truly am. I'm Ben Baker."

"Okay?" Then it hit him. "Holy shit, the president. The president of the United States, right? What the hell are...? What the heck are you doing here? In our house?"

"You said he'd not be dense about this. I was worried for a minute when he didn't know me." Addie told him to stop being an ass. "But you did tell me he'd be surprised that I was here."

"Don't be a moron, Ben. You know as well as I do that with you being in any house without a suit and tie, no one would know you. Also, he's not throwing a fit, like you said he would." Xander asked why he was supposed to throw a fit. "Because you're a wolf and he's a lion. Do you care?"

"No. I mean, so long as you're home and safe, he could be Satan himself for all I cared. I don't know if I'd be so welcoming, but there you have it." He looked at the tiger and Jamie. "What's going on, if I can know?"

Ben, as he insisted they all call him, laughed. "Addie here

is one of my top-notch workers for the CIA. I know what she is and all that and figured that her job set was perfect for what I needed. A hitman. However, I had no idea that others would try and use her for the same."

"Boone." He nodded. "What's going on with that? I'm assuming, since you're here and Jamie is too, that you didn't order the hit on the man as we've been told. I have no idea why I thought that. But it's been running around in my head for a few days now. The fact that the Feds ordered the hit and Addie is not being.... Never mind. You didn't order the hit, did you?"

"No, I did not. I wanted him to bring out the others, the men that he worked with, and get them all in a clean sweep. I didn't care at all if he should get himself murdered, I just didn't want it done at my doorstep, so to speak." Xander nodded. "I'm to understand that you have a special kind of help too. The wolf at the door."

"Asim. Yes. Why?" He told him. "Well, I think that's a good thing, don't you? I mean, your men did come into our home, busting down our door. If she has them shivering in their boots, then they're very lucky that she didn't kill them all. I don't care all that much for having guns pointed at my head, nor do I care to have my door busted open either."

Ben laughed. "You're a perfect match for Addie, I think. Has she told you that she works for me?" Addie said that she didn't work for him at all. "Yes, my dear, you do. So long as you work for a government agency that I oversee, then you work for me. I came to Jamie's aid a few days ago. This is the first time I was able to get away so that I could bring her here. Where I'm assuming that she'll be safe. Right?"

"Jamie couldn't be in safer hands than in my house. Especially with Addie here. As you're aware, she's the best there is." He heard the men downstairs and thought perhaps they were making themselves useful to Grayson. "They break anything, and they will fix or replace it."

They talked about the contract and the way that things were set up. The same name kept coming up — Finch. Or as Jamie called him, Birdman. The things that the man was in trouble for was a long laundry list that didn't look to Xander like it would ever wash out.

"I'm not making a move on him just yet, because to be honest with you, I haven't any idea what he's doing all this for. Yes, I can understand that Boone did need to be taken off the streets. And there was trouble in the offices before he came around. Also, and this is just between us, I think Finch is responsible for the deaths of Agents Conair, Cody, and Farquhar. I just don't know how or why yet." Xander wasn't sure that he knew the right answer, but he might have one. When he cleared his throat, Ben laughed again. "Go ahead, son. I think some fresh eyes would do us all a world of good."

"He's very good at that too." Addie explained how he'd figured out the numbers that had been given to her.

"I guessed, to be honest. And the numbers looked like something we learned in Boy Scouts, in learning to read a map. But that's a story for another time. What if he killed the three of them because of the contract that you can't find?" He asked him why he'd jumped to that conclusion. "Jamie. You said yourself that you didn't think that Farquhar would have hung himself. He had a lot going for him, and he was happy being on the job. Cody didn't drive."

"How did you know that?" Xander looked at Asim, who was sitting near the fireplace in the office, where they had all moved. "This sigil of yours, what else can it do that we can use? I do not want this to get out that we have someone in the justice department going off on his own agenda."

"I can have him take me to the bodies. Because of the nature of their deaths, none of the men have been buried."

Jamie stood up and handed her father, who was a big man now, the bag that she'd gotten from a faerie, she told them. "If he can get in and out without any trouble, he can take me there too. With my abilities to fit in the bag, no one will be the wiser. Now, I know that we can't use this in a court of law, but it'll give us something to go on. At least lead us in the right direction."

No one wanted her to go. But her argument was too sound. Her logic was perfect. The magic would only allow her to use the bag. No one else would be able to load it, nor would they be able to slip inside of it. Her father had gotten her away in it, and that was the only reason that she was alive now. While everyone agreed that Bug would go with her, no one wanted her to go alone.

"I'll go, Xander." He looked at Charles. "I might only be a ghosty, but I can do a few things that will distract them people from finding her there. A little push here, a trip up there. You let me go with her and I'll keep them camera things off'n her too."

That settled it. Yes, Charles could be a little off in things, but he was as sharp as a tack when it came to playing with the lives of humans. When the bag was filled with a few things she might need from Gabe—like knives, sample kits, as well

89

as some evidence bags—she slipped herself into the bag like one might slip a long knife into a leather sheath. An arm entered the small bag. Then her head after that, with the rest of her body following. Charles went ahead of her to *scoop*— his word, not theirs—and make sure she was "gonna be fine as rain."

Within half an hour, maybe a little more, she returned with all they needed and then some. She'd taken a little piece of clothing from each of them to smell. To her, she said, it smelled of meds, but she was sure, Jamie told them, that they could sort that out and use that as well.

He hoped so. Xander didn't want anyone hurt. And while he couldn't die, not since Addie had come into his life, he didn't care all that much for pain.

About the time they were ready to get to work, the men showed up to disembowel his basement.

~*~

Seasoned men were sickened by the smell. It wasn't that bad, not really, so Addie figured that it had more to do with the shape the body was in. Sharon had suffered at the hands of the man who had killed her and done so for a very long time.

"I don't think she was tossed down the stairs, do you?" She told Xander that she didn't think so. "The coroner thinks there might have been a child as well. This would be the second one this man murdered. The others were in the pool."

"I think this is why she didn't want to be brought up with her daughter around. Not only because there was a lot more damage done to her body than she said, but also the child. If there is one." Xander held her. "You know, before you came

90

along and held me, I could have gone my whole life without having another person touch me. And now, I don't just like it a great deal, but I find myself needing it more and more."

"Good. Because I find myself needing you more and more." They watched as the men continued to dig well after the body had been removed. What they found next startled him. Not just for what it was, but what it meant. "That's one of my brother's trunks, I'm thinking."

"Yes, it looks like the others. I'm almost afraid to open it." He said that they'd have to claim it, no matter what it was, because they knew about it. "I can maybe get that part taken care of. Just don't say anything about the others. That way, your brother is in the clear."

They had nothing to worry about. The trunk had nothing to do with the others on the property of Gabe, and more to do with the man he'd bought the house from. Not only did it have cash in it, from this century, but it also had fake identification, passports, as well as a sealed bag of clothing and keys to a car. It was a running trunk. But why it was under the basement was beyond her. It wasn't as if he could have gotten to it easily. But Charles knew the reason.

"I found those things, and me and the miss there, we put it all in there. Took her durn near a month for her to get that hole deep enough. I think she was thinking her days were counting off. I sure did miss having her around." Xander asked if she could see him. "Nah, not see me, but I got myself some of those there colored pencils and I could draw her stuff. She was a kind woman. And after a bit, when she was here, I helped her find a way to take care of her little girl. That Penny, she's all shiny like one, don't you think?"

91

"Yes, she is." They watched the trunk being inventoried, and the story that Xander told was that he could smell something off—not really a body, he assured them, but something like mildew. No one believed that was it, but they also knew better than to say anything. They had a murder solved, and that was just fine with them.

Xander sat with Addie in the kitchen as the rest of the basement was cleaned up.

"I heard from your mom a bit ago. She said that Penny is in need of new clothing, as well as a few girly things. I didn't ask what that meant." Xander told her that it was probably a good thing. "I'm not so sure. I have to go there. To the mall. Where there are people."

"That's usually— You are leaving your guns here, aren't you? I've had enough going on with the police today, if you don't mind." Addie laughed. He was so serious. But all she promised him was that she'd not kill anyone that didn't deserve it. "Define that for me. Who would deserve to be killed in a mall, shopping, for little girl's clothing?"

"She's twelve, Xander. If you call her a little girl, I'm afraid that you're going to be the worst dad ever born." He claimed he was all right with that. "No, you're not. And we both know it. Anyway, I'm to meet them at the mall and finish up with dinner. You're supposed to call your dad and get together with him. Apparently, he wanted to go too."

"Yes, I can see Dad wanting to go shopping for a little...a young woman. He's only ever had to shop for boys since we all were born. And since she's his first granddaughter that's born right now, he'd want to eat that up." Ben joined them in the room. Xander sat up straighter in his chair, and she might have laughed but she found herself standing taller too. "This man, the one coming for Addie and Jamie. What are you doing about keeping these men here from not saying anything?"

"Rogers." The name was bellowed through the house, and Addie was sure that the neighbors might have heard Ben say it. When the presumed Rogers came into the room, Ben asked him two questions. "Where are we? And what are we doing here?"

"We're nowhere but on the estate, sir. And we're not here. Haven't been here, nor will we allow anyone in this party to say a word to the contrary." He looked right at her. "Agent Dyer, I have a question for you too, if you would allow it."

"Sure. But know this—if you ask me anything personal, you are so not going to like the answer." He nodded. "Also, the answer is no, if you're asking me out. It's Mrs. Winchester now."

"Yes, ma'am, and congratulations to you both. But my question is, do you think you'd be interested in coming to the shooting range sometime and working with the newer recruits? When you were there with me, I think...no, I *know* that you made me a better shot with your...your methods."

"Methods? What did you do to that poor team?" Both Rogers and Addie laughed. Ben sat down as he continued. "Oh, now I have to know what is going on."

"She's very intense." Xander said he knew that about her. "Well, sirs, when we were on the range, a few of us weren't having any troubles with shooting the targets. We were kind of cocky about it to the others. And not only did she take us down a few notches, she showed us the error of our ways by helping us with shooting in a war zone."

"How?" She grinned at Xander when he asked. "You shot at them, didn't you? If so, then you are definitely leaving your gun here before going to the mall."

"No, sir, she didn't shoot at us. Though I'm betting that some of us wished that she had. She brought in a group of men—seasoned, you'd call them—and they took us down, one at a time, while we did practice ops with blanks in our guns. It was extremely frightening, but at the same time highly educational." Both Ben and Xander looked at her while Rogers continued. "She didn't ask us any names—we didn't know hers either. But one by one, the men would come to us and knock us around, until we were good at not just firing, but also reloading our weapons. In the month that she worked with us, not a one of us quit, we didn't whine, nor did we know when she was going to show up with her men."

"They needed a little tweaking, that's all." Rogers laughed. "What? That's all you needed. And if you say any differently, I'm going to pop you in the back of the head like Xander's mother does. It hurts, too."

She made her way to the mall. Addie was no longer worried about Finch, but she was worried for Jamie. Jamie wasn't hurt in any way, but she was disenchanted with her life because of her job. It would take her some time to come to the realization that people rarely did things because it was the right thing to do. No, most of the time, Addie had come to realize, people did whatever they wanted so long as it would profit them. Not all people, just a great many of them.

The two of them were going to have to get together soon. Not that she was a drinking/dancing sort of person, because that would include people, but she'd do it for her friend.

Sometimes, she knew, you had to upset your own life to help someone else out of their funk. And Jamie was in one.

The mall was busier than she'd thought it would be. People were everywhere, and it wasn't until she realized that it was close to Christmas that she put it together. Next month would be Thanksgiving, then after that a short thirty days until Christmas. She didn't have any idea how the Winchesters celebrated it, and knew that they would be going all out, as they did everything.

She found them in a shop so colorful and so loud that she was sure she'd have to have her ears checked when finished. And after one look at the women, she knew that things were not going well. When Penny saw her, she hugged her tightly and asked if she could just go home.

"Nope. And you know why." She nodded and started to turn away, but Addie stopped her. "Is this what you want? To shop here?"

She looked around and at the three women that were with her. Penny looked up at her and shook her head while tears streamed down her cheeks. Addie felt her heart crumble. Not just for her newly acquired daughter, but the people with her. None of them, it appeared, were having a good time here.

"Have you guys had lunch?" Sara looked as if she had handed her a lifeline and started hustling everyone together and out the door. Before she could suggest pizza or something like that, they were sitting in a lovely little bistro and having tea delivered to their table. "I was going to suggest that we ask Penny what she wanted."

"Oh, we did earlier. She was so in love with this place that we told her we'd take her here." Penny nodded and looked a little brighter than she had in the store. "I love the Reuben they have here. As well as the sweet potato fries. Actually, I don't think I've ever gotten a bad meal here."

After they all ordered, each a different thing, they started talking about shops. Quinn asked Penny want she wanted to wear, and she looked right at Addie. It was telling, that look, like she was drowning and wasn't sure anyone cared if she got a life jacket or not.

"Where did your mom take you to shop?" She told her. "Okay. We could go there, but I have a feeling that you're going to enjoy something nicer than that store can offer you. While I'm sure that they have good things there, Xander is making good money and only wants the best for you."

"What about you? Do you need something pretty too?" The women turned to stare at Penny with strange smiles on their faces as she spoke to Addie. "You should get pretty dresses to wear. And some nicer jeans. Those have big holes in them. If I have to shop, so do you."

"You've been hanging out with your grandma too much." They all laughed with Addie just as the food was being set before them. "All right, missy, one dress. But you have to get yourself something for school. It's high time we both looked like Winchesters."

The rest of the day was spent trying on clothing. Ignoring the stares they got—and they got plenty of them—Addie had a good time. There was a lot of snacking going on as well, from pretzels to ice cream. There was nothing nutritional, nor were they very calorie conscious. It was, she thought, one of the best days she'd had in a very long time. And she'd done it all without ever drawing her weapon. To her, that was a gold medal experience.

Chapter 6

The boys, his sons, were having a good time, but all Kelley could think about was having a little girl out there that might need him. He was sure that she was around the most protective women there were about, but he wanted to be her knight in shining, or even tarnished, armor. So, when the cars pulled into the drive, he was the first one out the door and making his way to them all.

"You buy much?" Sara handed him several bags, all of them from different shops. "My goodness. Is this all for one little girl?"

He winked at Penny and she hugged him. Kelley thought for sure he could get used to that sort of thing very quickly. And with the other boys having themselves little girls, he was going to be in high heaven soon. Penny was going to be his practice granddaughter and his favorite, he didn't mind thinking.

"I got the prettiest coat, Grandpa. You should see it. It's

dark blue with lots of fur around the hood. And some poop kicker boots like Addie wears. She doesn't call them that, but I can't say that word, so I just say poop kickers. And we had lunch in a big fancy restaurant, where I got to order from the menu all by myself. And Addie and I paid our own check, but Grandma was mad, so we let her leave the tip. Addie said it was too much, but Grandma said that putting up with her for an hour was hard work. I don't know what—" He put his finger to her lips and she smiled at him. "I'm talking a lot, huh?"

"Yes, you are, but that's all right with me. I was wondering if you got yourself a dress or something equally pretty I can see you in."

He got an "Oh, Grandpa" before she flounced—actually flounced—away, and he noticed that someone had cut her hair. "What did you do to my sweet little granddaughter?"

Kelley wasn't aiming his question at anyone in particular. He didn't want his butt kicked either. But someone had to explain to him why she was wearing a dark blue coat and poop kickers. He then noticed that he was standing there with several bags in his hand, and he was out there all by himself with Addie. He nearly ran off when she said his name.

"I'm going to be her stepmom soon." He nodded, not sure what to think of the awe in her voice. "I know nothing of children. Less about girls. But I figured that since she and I were so new to each other, we should make this more about her and not about pink. Do you understand?"

"Yes. I suppose I might. I just thought, you know, that she'd be a pretty little girl a lot longer. You know, might need me for a bit to slay dragons." She told him that when a dragon came to visit, she'd make sure that he could pretend to kill it. "I'm not sure if you're joking or not."

"I'm not. But back to Penny. She doesn't know how to be a girly girl. And neither do I. Thankfully, your wife is girly enough for all of us. There are dresses in those bags, as well as panties—not underwear—and bras." He said he didn't need to know that. "Yes, you do, Kelley. And there is more you need to know. She loves you like someone that she can worship on a daily basis. But I'm serious about this. I'm going to need your help on how to be a good mom."

"You can depend on me, I promise you. And I surely do like that she loves me, but I think there might be more." She nodded. "You tell me, girl, and I'll fix it up for you. Unless you want me to tell my pretty wife that you don't want to shop anymore. I think that it would break her heart to hear that."

"No, nothing like that. But it's about the holidays. I haven't any idea how to do that." Kelley asked her what she meant. "Well, do you put up a tree? Are there gifts for everyone, including the adults? I've been around since long before there was a reason to celebrate the season, Kelley, and I haven't ever had a tree or anything that goes with it."

"Never? You've never.... My goodness. We're going to have to fix that, aren't we?" She said that's what she was hoping for. "Good gravy. We have to get some...ornaments. That's what they were talking about tonight. Ain't a one of them got any other than the few that their momma gave them as kids. I didn't even.... Goodness gracious, I got some shopping to do now too."

He was nearly to the house when he realized that he'd just

walked away from her. Glancing at the young woman—well, young looking woman—he realized what she'd said to him. She'd been around before they'd had a reason to celebrate the season. Sitting on the porch steps, he wasn't surprised when she came over and sat next to him.

"I'm not sure what I said that has that look on your face, but I can assure you, I meant nothing about it." He asked her about her age. "Ah, yes, that's about how old I am. Older actually."

"I didn't know." She nodded. "Does Xander know how old you are? Or have any idea how long you've been around?"

"Yes, he does, and it freaks him out." He nodded, seeing that about his kid. "Kelley, may I ask you a question? About yourself and Sara?"

"Sure 'nough. But I have to tell you, I ain't as honest as you might be, girl. Holy jingle bells, I surely ain't." They both laughed, and Kelley put his hand on her leg, just for the contact for a moment. "When the boys were wee little ones, me and my darlin', we was so poor that we'd not been able to rub two nickels together to come up with a dime. Then one day, my boy Caleb, he nearly killed himself to avoid hitting a man by the name of Cartwright with our truck. Cartwright was in a poor way, what with his wife passing and all. And he wanted Caleb to hit him, send him off to be with her."

"Xander said that he made it so that they'd all be able to go to college, as well as that he came to dinner nearly every night." Kelley told her he was a good friend. "What brought him up, Kelley?"

"Nothing really. And everything. He was so rich that we'd not have had him over if we'd known that. I suppose that was the reason he didn't tell us. But he didn't care, I'm guessing. Dinner was just that with him around. And Christmas was special too with him. He didn't go overboard, show off 'cause he could afford more than we could. He'd give the boys some money and a few things of clothing. And when they graduated from high school, he'd give them a little more. But college, that was a big deal to him." He grinned at her. "Sorry, my dear, what was it you wanted to ask me?"

"It's more like a question that was put to me. And before you get your buttons all snapped off, listen to my entire story." He nodded. Kelley did like this woman. "I've been asked to head up the FBI. As well as have input to the CIA. That'll means that I have to move out there, or at least have a house there, so I can go and work a few times a week. At least until after they get things back to the way that they should be."

"You're thinking of not taking it." She nodded at him, excitement and happiness all over her face. "I see now. You do know that we'd miss you something terrible. And not to mention, that little girl of yours. But we got our own limo now — had to convince me of that purchase. And a plane that we needed too when things started to go for Caleb and Owen. I'm sure going to put some use to it when it gets a bit warmer. Plus, there is the added fact that Xander can do what he does just about anywhere. So, I don't see why you don't want to take it."

"As you said, you'd miss my little girl, as well as your son." He asked her if she thought he'd miss her. "You don't know me well enough to miss me yet. And before you say that you would, I'm talking on the same level as you would miss Xander and Penny."

"I'd miss you the same. If not more. You done went and put a big part of my heart on hold just for you. And every time you come around or I get to have a conversation with you, like this one here, I feel like your part of me just deepens. The others, the other girls, they sure have a hunk of me too, but you're more.... I want to say that you're more protective of me and my ticker." He looked at her, wondering if he was fudging things up with her. "I'm a man of simple needs, Addie. I love like it's my business. Hug like I'm never gonna see you again, and when I'm happy, which is pert near all the time now, I want all those around me to feel the same way. And you and the others, you give me that."

"Kelley Winchester, I think you're about the sweetest and most wonderful person, shifter or otherwise, that I've ever met in my life. And since you know that's a very long time, you know that it's true." He nodded and pulled out his big hankie. "You and your handkerchiefs. I swear, they get bigger all the time."

"Well, I tell you. I have two." He pulled the second one out that was smaller. "This one is for my nose. I get me a powerful nose full of snot when I'm working. And this one is for my happiness. I have them in different sizes for a reason."

He waited on her to get it. And when she did, he nearly fell off the porch with her when she just threw back her head and laughed like she meant it. Kelley was sure enough that it was the best sound that he'd ever heard. Besides his wife telling him that she loved him.

Getting up, he gave her his hand and helped her to stand. Entering the house, he was pleased to see his granddaughter standing there in the prettiest pink flowered dress. The boots, the poop kickers, weren't his idea of matching the mood, but he was happy that she'd done this for him. Hugging her tightly, he kissed the top of her head and told her that he loved her.

"You really do?" He touched his finger to her nose and told her forever. "Oh Grandpa, that's the best news. I'm going to go out to dinner with you. Grandma said that you and I needed girly time."

"She did, did she? Well, hot dog with mustard, I'm thrilled as I can be." He looked at her boots and then at her. "Go on now, get your coat. Do you have a purse? Get that too if you do."

When she ran up the stairs, he pulled out his large hankie. When he was finished with it, he handed it to Addie. Yes, sir, he was surely going to love having these women and little girls around him for the rest of his life.

"Kelley, I've given her some money." He told his Sara that he'd pay. "I know that, poop head, I mean for her to buy you dessert. And don't you dare say a word about her not paying for it either. She needs to feel free."

He wanted to protest, but he closed his mouth when he looked over at Xander. He was shaking his head, little like, and he told his Sara that he'd not say a word. Walking to his son, he asked him if he was all right with that and Xander hugged him. When Penny came back down the stairs, Xander stood on the third step with his love and cleared his throat. Kelley didn't know what was going to be his announcement, but whatever it was, he could see the happiness all over his face.

~*~

105

Xander pulled out the press release that he'd received yesterday via courier. He cleared his throat again and looked over at Addie when she laughed. He told her that he could do this, announce to his family, but now that he was here to do it, he just shoved it at her and let her do the honors.

"The book, *Talking with a Dead Man*, written by Xander Winchester, will start production soon to be a full-fledged movie for the big screen. The story is about a man, Charles Winston, and his adventures during a time in our lives that no one has written better than Mr. Winchester."

"Whoa your ponies there, girl. What do you mean, that dead man book is in production?" She grinned at him and Xander looked at his dad as he continued. "I didn't even know that you'd done and finished it."

"It's hitting the markets tomorrow, as a matter of fact. I had them release it on Penny's birthday." Everyone looked at the little girl, his little girl, and she buried her head in his side. "My publisher said it was the best book she'd ever read, and after making a few calls and sending out scripts of it, a big Hollywood producer called her back and I was made a deal." No one said a word and he explained more. "I haven't cashed the check yet. I was worried that she'd say that he'd changed his mind and that it would have to be returned. Besides, I wasn't even sure how to cash the check. I've never seen so many —"

"How long have you known about this?" His mom sounded so disappointed that he felt his heart race. "I'm not the least bit surprised that it's going to be a movie. You did write it."

"Yes, well, I had to make sure that she wasn't doing this

106

because she'd been paid to do so." Again, the silence was too loud for him. "She told me that had it come across her desk for her to publish, even without Mr. Cartwrights asking her to do so, she would have published it anyway. She told me that it was that good. As for the movie rights, she said that it was really a great book and she is working on getting the best possible deal for me. For us. And she did."

He held out the check, and told them that it was only a portion of what he was going to get for the book. Xander was also going to get a percentage of the movie profits, as well as the DVD rights. This was the best possible deal, he told them.

"I'm so proud of you that I could just about bust." He was relieved when his mom came to him and hugged him. Then it was like a sign had been held up for everyone to speak. But he thought that Dominic had summed it up about the best way.

"For a dummy, you sure did good."

After his dad and Penny left for dinner, he took his family to the basement to show them what he had to fix now. It wasn't as bad as he'd thought it would be. Nor was it going to be closed soon. The police had asked him to wait.

"What are you saying to Penny?" He told Caleb that she'd known her mother was going to be found. "Yes, but there is a child involved. She will need to know that as well. And not only that, but the other items there as well. Otherwise, she'll see it in the paper. Maybe not today or this year, but she'll need to know."

Xander agreed, but he wasn't sure how he should go about it either. He looked at his mom when she said his name. She was crying.

"She knows about the baby. And that her mom is at

peace. She just told her grandda. They're pulled to the side of the road now so that he can hold her. I'm so glad that the old fool was able to do this for her. They'll be closer than ever now." He wasn't sure if his mom was slightly jealous of that, but he hugged her. "I tell you, there are days when I'd gladly strangle the man, then there are days when I just want to hug him to my heart and keep him there."

"I know, Mom. I know just how you feel." He held her while she cried too. It was difficult for them all, this emotional rollercoaster ride they were on. What with all the crap going on and something new every day, Xander was beginning to feel like the ride was too much for him and he needed to step back. "Mom, I have an idea."

She looked up at him. "Whatever it is, I'm for it." He kissed her cheek. "Now I know that I am. Please let it be good. I need something good right now."

"It's going to be epic. Let's see.... It's six weeks until Christmas, and two until Thanksgiving. We're going to have a huge dinner party with friends, every week for the next seven weeks. At each of our homes." She was nodding, and he could see her mind already working. "It doesn't have to be a meal each time."

"Oh, but it does. And at each house, the staff from the others will come and have a meal with us too. No, no, no. We'll hire someone to come in and serve. The staff will cook from each home, and then be served at the house. Oh, I love this." She walked away, then turned back when she was on the first step to go upstairs. "Well? Come on. We have a lot to plan if we're going to make this work."

And work they did. Each of his brothers had their own

home and a cook. Before they started on how to cook it, they got with his cook, Skyler, and asked him what he thought.

"Oh, my Lord, this will be great. We were just wondering how we were going to plan meals. What day of the week would you like to have it on? I would suggest Saturdays. That way no one misses the shopping day for that Friday, and we can be with our own families on the big days." Xander asked him to get with the others and find out. In half an hour, he was back and beaming. "Yes, Saturday would suit us if it does you. And Ms. Snow said that each of us should make a meal that we enjoy the most."

Before they left for the night, his brothers had their assignments. Xander thought for sure that Tyler was going to not want to do this, because of his comments about not having a wife, but he soon joined in the hullaballoo and was putting in suggestions too. Then it came to order of dinners.

"I'll start. That way I can enjoy my sons' meals much better. And I'll have time to put up my tree afterwards. We're still meeting at your dad's and my house, correct, for Christmas morning?" In unison they said yes to Sara. "Good. This will be my first Christmas with grandchildren, and I aim to spoil them rotten. This first time."

Xander, as well as the rest of them, knew that Mom and Dad were going to spoil all the kids every year, but it didn't seem to bother them overly much. They'd not harm them with their spoiling, that he was sure of.

"You guys acted like this was a statement of war you were putting together." Xander laughed when Addie joined him on the couch. "Your dad just called. Your mom is going to meet him in town and they're going to take Penny to the movies before coming back here. I guess Penny and Kelley had a wonderful time. And she was able to buy him ice cream afterwards. I had no idea your dad liked ice cream so much."

"Yes. Even when we were dirt poor, we'd find a way to have it, mostly it was homemade. Mom would barter with the man who lived down the street for some of his cream, and she'd give him a pie or two. It was a good deal for us all." He thought about ice cream. "In the spring we'd have strawberry, summer would mean blueberry. And in the fall, she'd fry up some apples and freeze them before dumping them in the creamy mixture. Sometimes we'd just have vanilla, but there was usually some kind of fruit to go with it."

They sat on the couch until their bodies seemed to entwine. He was never sure if it was her or him that kissed first, but almost as soon as their mouths came together, so did their bodies ignite.

Making love to Addie was never just sex. It was a marathonic race to see who could come the hardest and the fastest, while satisfying the other partner several times before the bell rang. And boy oh boy, did his bell ever ring. There were times when he was sure that she'd killed him. Or at least she was giving it her best shot.

When they tumbled to the floor, she sat over him, their clothing once again in tatters all around them. She had a way about her that made him want her to tear into his body, and he supposed for them both, it was safer for her to rip apart jeans instead. When she was riding him hard and fast, Xander sat up and roughly pulled her nipple into his mouth. When she cried out she was coming, he suckled at her harder, wanting to give her a little bit of the overwhelming sex that she gave

110

him.

"Xander, Christ, you're going to make me come again like this." He laughed and told her to go ahead. "I want to come with you in my mouth. You have no idea how satisfying that is for me."

"Let me come deep inside of you, love. Fill you with all that I am." When he got no answer, he rolled her to her back and looked down at her and stopped moving. "You are the most beautiful creature I've ever seen. And I love you with all my heart."

"I love you as well."

Slowing down his body, making his hands touch instead of grab, he told her what he was feeling, how her skin felt in his hands. How much he loved her taste.

"Xander, you're almost too much for me when you make love to me like this, it's like you're consuming me, and while I enjoy it immensely, it's almost too much."

"Well, that's too bad." He kissed her before she could protest. "You're the best thing that has ever happened to me. I love the way you make me laugh at myself. The way that you only need to look at me and I can tell what you think of what I have on."

"You do the same to me. I love you." She said it over and over as he continued to tell her things, touching her softly and with reverence. "I want you to marry me, Xander. Forever. I want to bear your children, have your name, and let everyone know that you and I are together forever."

He had proposed to her several times over the last few days, but her answer had always been the same. Later, when we have time. Or that they didn't need to marry, they were content the way things were now.

"Yes, I'll marry you." She laughed, then bowed up from the floor, her nails dug deep into his back so hard that he felt blood trickle down his body. And when his own climax took him, he came hard enough that he was sure that not only did his eyes roll to the back of his head, but that they might have ended up someplace where his feet were. Throwing back his head, he howled out his release as his wolf seemed to know that she'd taken them both to levels that they'd never been before.

"I love you."

He picked her up when he could walk. The stairs were too much tonight, he thought with a small grin. Xander finally had enough that he simply threw her over his shoulder like a sack of potatoes and carried her up that way. Tossing her on the bed made it shatter beneath her. Laughing harder now, he joined her on the broken wood and closed his eyes. If he never woke again, he'd be thrilled with that.

Chapter 7

Jamie knew she was being followed, but who it was, she didn't know. Her dad had left the day before yesterday with the promise that he'd be back soon. Well, she wasn't going to let people bully her again. Today, she was going to make sure that everyone knew that she was a fucking CIA agent, and they were not going to fuck with her. Channeling Addie, Jamie turned to the man and asked him what the fuck he was doing.

"You knew I was following you?" Taking someone to the ground had never been more fun. She didn't know him or why he was following her, but there wasn't any way she was going to be a sap again. "Miss? You don't seem to understand. Ouch, that fucking hurt."

Making him cry out again made her feel good. Then she felt terrible when he begged her to allow him to speak. Letting him go, she stood over him when he put his hands on his head and didn't stand. Something made her think he was waiting

113

for someone to help him when he grabbed her around the waist suddenly and pulled her under him.

Struggling to be let go, she heard the glass shatter just beyond where they were. When he begged her again, this time to stay down, she nodded. It wasn't until she saw his gun that she remembered that she was armed as well. With a quick kiss to her mouth he left her there, thinking.... Well, she wasn't thinking, that was what was wrong.

Kneeling behind the car about ten yards from where she was, Jamie pulled out her gun and shot the man who had fired at her. When he screamed she heard another shot—this one felled a man in the second story window of the office building across the street. When the man who had followed her came back, he put out his hand then jerked it back before she could take it.

Standing, she glared at him. "Are you this rude all the time?" He told her he wasn't normally, no. "So, it's must be just me."

"Yes. And who you are. I'm Taylor Warren. You're the leap leader's daughter, Jamie Riddell." She nodded. "I didn't want to touch you just yet, because you're my mate. I'm sorry about that."

"Sorry that you didn't touch me, or sorry about being your mate? Because from where I'm standing, I'm not sure I'd like being your mate any more than you do me. You're a rude bastard, and don't you think I won't tell my father about your ill treatment of—"

She was jerked to him and kissed like he meant to mark her. Wrapping her arms around him as he deepened the kiss, Jamie held onto him for dear life. It was that or melt into a puddle of over-sexed hormones. When he pulled back, holding onto her, she did the only thing she could think of. Jamie pulled him close again and kissed him right back.

The kiss was more than she'd ever had. Not that many men had kissed her. She was the type to have men eating out of her palm simply because she had made them afraid of her. It was the way she liked it, the way that she wanted it. Until this man came along.

Letting him go, she still stood in his arms while he looked down at her. Taylor was much taller than her own six-foot frame, and that, for odd sexual reasons, pleased her greatly. She asked him if he was all right when he continued to stare at her.

"I think so. Are you?" She answered him the same. "Yeah, that's about right. I was supposed to help out the leader by keeping an eye on you. It wasn't until you stopped and turned that I caught your scent."

"I'm usually very careful about always wearing too much perfume, but my dad, it makes him sneeze and I forgot." He asked her why she'd do that. "To make it so no one knows that I'm a cat. I just...it's dangerous in my line of work."

"I would imagine. Can I kiss you again?" She nodded, and he did so, this time pressing his erection into her softer fold. "Christ, I had no idea that you'd be the one. Not that I care who you are, but your father, he's going to murder me."

"Why would he do that?" With a sexy grin, he told her. "Oh. Yes, he might be angry at you for taking my virginity. But once he figures out that we're a mated couple, then he'll not hurt you too much."

"It's the not too much that I'm worried about." They both

115

laughed this time. "You're very beautiful. But the police are coming, so we have to at least act like we're concerned that these men are dead, don't you think?"

Jamie pulled out her badge and was surprised when Taylor did as well. While hers hung from her belt, his was on a chain that hung around his neck. The letters FBI made her skin run cold and her body freeze nearly solid.

You are distant now. What's happened? She told him nothing, that this had been a mistake. *Jamie, come here to me and explain.*

No, I like you just where you are. You're with the FBI. You must know this guy that's your boss. I hate him. He asked her what his name was and what he'd done to her. *You know, I might have been the bad guy in all this. Why do you sound as if you know it was him and not me that's the terrible person? But his name is Lyman Finch. I call him Birdman.*

Yes, I know him, but I don't work for him. I'm from the presidential task force that works on international situations. And I know who you are, as well as about Addie. She is on the FBI list of known assailants. She told him what she knew, not revealing that Addie was only at the grocery store a block or two away. *We have had Birdman, which I have to admit, suits the little fucker, in our sights for some time now. He's a playboy that tries to play in the big leagues, but has found himself lacking. He's also in trouble about some women that he hurt.*

He tried to hurt me. He said that he'd been aware of him hurting a woman, but not that it was her. *I'm not the only one either. Addie.* He asked her.... *I'm sure you've heard.*

Yes, all of it. President Baker asked me to come here to keep an eye on things, and to watch out for Birdman. And since I was here, your father, a nice man by the way, asked me if I would keep an eye out for you as well. I'm not sure that Birdman would be smart enough to try anything with either of you after seeing you in action. And had he seen you a few minutes ago, he would stay away. But the problem is, I don't think he's all that smart.

He's not. The police seemed to be at a loss as to why someone would try and kill them. What they really said was that someone had shot at them, not the killing part. *We're going to end up in jail or prison if we can't get these people to believe us here.*

I'm sure soon that they'll have their shit together.

She wasn't so sure and said as much. But just as she was ready to draw her gun and fire in the air, just to get their attention and make them focus, she saw Caleb coming toward them.

One of the officers dropped to the ground; another stood his ground, but looked like he'd take off if anyone said anything to him. Or he'd wet himself. Then she saw the anger on Caleb's face. He wore it like a mantel, like this was his game face and he wasn't going to take any prisoners today. If he ever had.

"What the blue fuck is going on around here?" The second man did drop then, and rolled to his back to show his belly. "Get up, you moron. This is a public forum. What the hell are you doing detaining the FBI and the CIA? Did you not read what their badges said?"

"We were told to hold them." Caleb asked by who. "Agent Finch. He's on his way here. He said that if we had any trouble with the CIA, we was to call him right away and he'd come talk to them. Something about an unsolved murder of Agent Riddell."

"In the event you didn't notice, I'm not murdered." She clicked her tongue at them. "You know, I think Mr. Winchester is right, you are morons. And that guy over there, Agent Warren? Why is he being detained? Or is he supposed to be held because he's.... Wait, he can't be with me, I'm fucking dead." The last words were shouted at them, and each of them, human and wolf, whimpered.

Taylor came to stand next to her, but he didn't try to take over nor did he touch her. She was both upset with that and glad. If he touched her, he'd be taking her thunder away. And right now, she was on a roll.

After demanding that they give her any contact information on Birdman—they snickered when she called Finch that—she handed it off to Taylor. As he dealt with that, she waited for her father.

Taylor told her that he wasn't going to speak to the men, not after she told him what had gone down. But he wanted to be close to her, to make sure that no one else was helping Birdman.

"What's the plan?" She glanced up at Taylor and her mind went blank. "You keep looking at me like that, and not only will there not be a plan from you, but you'll be gone for a long time before your father shows up. Now, calmly, without making me insane to have you, let out a long breath and think."

Inhaling deeply, she could smell Taylor and what he meant to her. He was a strong cat, like her father was. He would, more than likely, take over a leap one day if he didn't have one already. But when she let out her breath, he moaned, and that made her less focused on her job again. But without

118

Birdman in custody, they were all fucked.

"I need to catch Birdman at his worst." He asked her how she was going to do that. "I don't know yet. I don't suppose you have any ideas."

"Yes, two. And one of them has to do with you." She cocked a brow at him and he laughed. "Christ, I'm going to enjoy taking you to bed. I was thinking that we could use you as bait. That way—"

"You will not be using my little girl as bait for anyone." Taylor stepped in front of her, cutting her off from her dad. When he grabbed Taylor, more than likely to kill him, she slapped her father in the face. No one moved.

"Step back." He growled at her. "Dad so help me, if you don't step back, you're going to call my cat and we're all going to be fucked up."

"He is not going to use you as bait." She told him to let Taylor go. "Baby, you're pissing me off."

"Well, welcome to the club. Dad let my mate go." No one moved. Not her father nor Taylor. And in that moment, she knew that if pushed, Taylor could have killed her father. But he'd remained calm and in control when her dad had not. "He's my mate. The man you had following me, he's my mate."

She wasn't sure what was going through her dad's head. He looked shocked—so was she, Jamie supposed—but then all of a sudden, it was like a light had gone off and her dad was picking Taylor up, and she was sure that he was going to be killed.

"Welcome to the family." He set Taylor down, then hugged her in the same manner. "A man to keep you under control. Though if he's a smart man, which I believe that he is, then he won't try and corral you, but let you do what you do best. Be the best man there is."

"You're all right with this?" Dad asked Taylor why he thought he wouldn't be. "I don't know. I'm FBI, she's CIA. I'm a man, she's not."

"I'm well aware of what she is, young man. And I think what you're trying to tell me is, that you're a man with experience, and she is not." Taylor looked so relieved that she wanted to remind them both that she was still there. Instead, she simply walked away. She heard her dad's burst of laughter. Then Jamie saw Birdman.

The piece of shit car looked like it was older than he was. When he got out, his passenger did as well. Right away she knew that it was his father. From the pictures that she'd seen of the man, he looked ten times worse now than he had when it had been taken. Which, if she remembered correctly, was only about four years ago.

"There you are. I've been trying to locate you since you left work a few days ago. I've been covering for you." She asked him how he was doing that. "You know, telling your boss that you were injured and that you needed time off."

"I've spoken to my boss as well. He is well aware of me not being hurt, not unless you count you nearly jerking my arm out."

He looked to her right, and when he smiled, she turned too. "Hello, Mr. Warren. You seem to have forgotten to report to me when you're in my jurisdiction."

"No, I didn't." He didn't say more, and Jamie had to cover her mouth so as not to laugh at the expression on Birdman's face.

"Hello, boss."

~*~

Addie knew that the exchange between the two men was going to be heated. What she didn't expect and probably should have was the anger that was displayed on Birdman's face. It was as if he had expected to waltz in here, take over, and bring her back to a firing squad. Instead of speaking, this time she listened to the men. Listening, she thought, was one of her strongest suits.

"You? You've been popping up all over the place, haven't you, Mr. President?" The man from the car came barreling up to them and tried to push Birdman out of the way. "You'd almost think you were stalking me."

"I don't need to stalk, Birdman, I know where you are at all times." The elder man laughed, his face nearly purple with it. "You think you have something to say?"

"This is my idiot son, your honor." Ben said he wasn't anything but Mr. President. "All righty then. I'm the idiot's father, Leonardo Finch. I love that you call him Birdman. We'll have to do that at home as—"

"Dad, you were supposed to stay in the car. I'm here to retrieve Ms. Dyer and her partner, Ms. Riddell. They have some things to explain to me." Ben asked what that might be. "Well, for one thing, the murder of Mr. Boone. Then there are the deaths of several of my men when they tried to stop her from killing him."

"Really? That's the best you can do? Well, I have it on good authority that you ordered the hit. The men were there before she was. That shots were fired at her before she even

121

left her spot, and that you went above your own boss's head to make all this happen." Birdman said that was all lies. "Are you calling me a liar, Birdman?"

"My name is Agent Lyman Finch." He seemed to have remembered who he was speaking to. "I'm sorry, sir, but I don't think you have all the facts just right. I didn't have a contract with Ms. Dyer, nor did I contact her—"

"Agent." Birdman looked at her finally. "Suffix isn't Ms., nor is it Dyer. My name is Special Agent for the CIA, Adaline Winchester. And it would behoove you to remember that."

"Winchester? You mean those upstarts that have been harassing me all over town? Just the other afternoon, they told my father and me that I should—" His dad told him it was just him they'd told to leave town, not him or his other son, Leo. "One of them told me that my *family* and I should leave town before we were hurt. Of course, I chose to ignore that threat. Especially when I have a job to do."

"And just what is it your job to do?" Addie wanted to know what it was too. So, she waited with Ben for an answer. "You're required by law—law that I'm going to hold you to—to answer me. What is your job? Or better yet, what is the motto of your area?"

"Fidelity, bravery, and integrity." He seemed quite pleased with himself, and Ben turned to her and winked. Then he asked Birdman what the words meant. "Meaning? Well, fidelity is loyalty or trustworthiness, I guess. Bravery is.... Why does it matter if I know every little word in the motto?"

"It's only three words." Ben looked over at her. "You know them, don't you? And you're not even one of his men.

What are they, Addie?"

"Thank God, I'm not. As for what they mean? Fidelity stands for faithfulness and reliability. Bravery is courage and valor. Integrity is having dependability and honesty. The motto for the Central Intelligent Agency is The Work of a Nation. The Center of Intelligence." She stared right at Birdman. "The reason you should know them is, they were on the test. And your test score, if I remember correctly, was a hundred percent. You should have known them, you moron."

"Now see here—"

Whatever he was going to say was cut off. When she watched his face crumble with pain, Addie pulled both her knife and gun from under her shirt. The person standing on the back of a pickup truck that was starting up was putting his weapon down when Birdman took a tumble backward.

She didn't know the man nor the vehicle. When it sped away, she told Bug to follow as soon as he could. When he was in flight, she also saw Asim trailing alongside of the truck, and knew that sooner than she could have found them, they'd be caught.

"Shoulder wound." Addie waited for Taylor to tell her that he was surely going to die, but he only shook his head. "He'll make it. But his father is dead."

The bullet meant for someone else, she surmised, had done a through and through in the chest of Mr. Birdman—Finch, she supposed. Feeling for his pulse, just to be sure he was dead, the ruthlessness of the man himself was there for her to envision. Had he been anything like his son, she would have felt that too, but he was far worse—like hundreds of times worse.

He'd killed, she knew that too. And without mercy. Mr. Finch had also been brutal to his son, Lyman. Leo, however, was the favorite of the two of them, and his being in a wheelchair was the fault of his mother. An accident. But that wasn't the end of it. The accident had been terrible, but not nearly enough to have someone killed over it. And her death hadn't been easy. She'd been murdered, and quite heinously.

Birdman Senior had hired the two men to take Addie and then Lyman out of the picture. Why her, she didn't know, but she could see the reasons behind having Lyman killed. This family was really fucked up.

There were other things she could see in Birdman's head when she touched him, things that she knew he'd done in the name of his own self-proclaimed power trip. And then she saw the reason that he'd done all of this—because she had spurned Birdman when he'd asked her out. So long ago that she had very little memory of it now.

When the medic took him away, Birdman was still out. But she had enough information now, enough not just to have him put away, but also his brother. Had their father not died, he'd be right there with them. Prison might not be kind to Lyman, but it was going to be horrific for his brother.

"You all right?" She shook her head at Xander, then nodded. "I'm afraid of that, if you want to know the truth."

"So should Lyman and Leo Finch be." He asked her if he could help her. Pulling him to her, she kissed him like she might not see him again, and that was just how he took it. "I'm coming back, I promise, but I'm going to kick some ass while I'm gone. I think this has gone on long enough."

She spoke to Ben and told him what she'd found out. Not

124

all but most of it. There was one point, the sticking one, that she kept all to herself. And that, she knew, was going to be the most fun she'd ever had. Telling him what her plan was, she asked that both Taylor and Jamie go with her. Jamie was the best at electronics that she'd ever met.

"What can I do for you? I need to help."

She nodded and pulled Xander aside. This next conversation was for him and him alone. It wasn't until she was in a large SUV, which was moving as she got into it, that she realized that she was having fun again. It had been so long since she'd enjoyed her job that she had seriously considered quitting. As the car pulled away, she told them her plan. It was perfect, so long as nothing went wrong. Laughing, she wondered how much fun Xander was going to have, as well as Charles.

The old ghost had taken a shine to her, Xander told her. He wanted to just sit and talk to her, about the wars she'd seen, the people that she might have known. Charles asked Xander if he was going to write a book about her, and she told him not so long as she was an agent. And that she was unlike Jamie, who wanted to stay now that she'd found her mate. Jamie wanted babies and a nice quiet life at home. She was even going to grow a garden and plant flowers.

Addie wasn't a flower planting type of person. She was more of a trample them down sort of individual, and wearing a dress to anything other than a wedding or a funeral wasn't her thing either. But for her, like Jamie, there were dress blues that they wore. No dress, no stockings, and certainly no heels. That was what she wanted to do, be a service man, for as long as they'd let her.

The building had been a safe house at one time. Even now they used it for security purposes. Like Jamie had told her, it was state of the art shit that cost more than the entire block of buildings was worth. Going to the upper level, she saw that Jamie had already gotten to work on her request, and handed her a printout of the things she'd asked for.

What do you know of international taxes? She told Jamie that she knew nothing. *Yeah, me neither. Can you make some shit up?*

The two of them had exchanged blood a long time ago. Few knew that, Jamie's father being one that did. But as far as the rest of her team, the men that she or Jamie worked with, they hadn't a clue. While talking on the phone with each other, they could and did have long covert conversations that could get them both killed. Right now, Jamie was talking verbally about the house that she was going to purchase soon.

Make shit up about international taxes? Yes, you know that I can. What do you know? Jamie pointed to the last page of the document, and Addie decided that no matter how many stupid flowers she planted, Jamie wasn't leaving the service. *Where did you dig this up? And before you tell me, have a look around. This paperwork can be looked at by invisible eyes as good as what I can see.*

Yes, I'm aware of that. The cameras were everywhere in this place, and sound was recorded too. Even in the event of a power outage, there were enough generators running at all times that it would run after lights out for about ten years. *They can no more see them than I can the way you're facing.*

Holy fuck balls, Jamie. You're going before a firing squad if this isn't right. She told her that it was all true. *You were searching for this long before I asked you to have a look, weren't you?*

Yes, years. Since I joined up. Addie sat down, handing the paperwork to her. *Tell me what you can find out about the Winchesters. All of them. If what you found is true, they're as fucked as we are.*

No. No one can touch them. She asked her why not. *Because, my dear friend, you're going to throw the right people under the bus, and it'll turn out just fine and dandy.*

The rest of the afternoon and well into the morning was spent going over the things that just about everyone was aware of. The shooters had been dealt with after finding out who had hired them and why. The wolf pack had had their fun. And neither man would be found again. Even Asim and Bug had gotten in a few licks.

"The two men, what do you know about them?" Jamie handed her a sheet of paper that had some of the information that she could get on the two men, which honestly was very little compared to what she told her through their connection.

She had their bank statements, who had paid them and how much, as well as information on where they had spent most of their ill-gotten gains and a lot more. One of them had been thrifty, the other, not so much. In total, both men had been paid a total of sixty million in cash to not kill just her, as they had thought, but her and Taylor. The man had only just come on the scene, and she had a hard time equating the kind of money that was being put out there for him when it hit her.

Jamie, how many people, other than the few that work for you, knows that your first name is James? She said that no one knew as far as she knew. *Other than the few that have seen your application, correct?*

No. And had you not brought it up, I might not have remembered that as a lie. I put Jamie. She looked at Addie when what was going on occurred to her as well. *They think that Taylor is James. Not me, but him. They were aiming at him and you, right?*

Yes, that's what I believe as well. She handed her the paperwork and sat down. *I'm going to have to go home soon. I want you to come with me. Or at the very least to see Taylor. The two of you should be able to keep yourselves safe.*

Yes. She looked around the office again. "I'm going to look at houses tonight. This will be a good time to go look, since there is nothing here."

"I know. I surely thought there'd be more information."

Jamie stood up and picked up her purse. They were baiting the hook, as Kelley had said to her once. It was the catch of the day that scared her more than anything.

Chapter 8

This was going to be fun, or so he hoped. If Addie was wrong, he was going to look like such an asshole. Today, however, he was working for the CIA—in a diminished capacity, but he was still having a blast.

Going to the front door, he knocked hard. He was with Charles, though no one could see him but himself. And there was Gabe, as the local doctor, and Agent Warren. He was really going to like having the guy around now that he was accepted as Jamie's mate. He thought they could be good friends. Xander knocked again when there was no answer.

"You sure Leo is here?" Charles disappeared then came back, nodding. "You saw him? Don't tell me if he was in a compromising position."

"He was in a position, all right." Xander told him to shut up and he laughed. Telling Taylor what was going on, the man laughed too. The third knock got him a gun shoved in his belly in the hands of a pissed off man in a wheelchair.

129

"Who the fuck are you? And what are you doing here this early in the morning?" Looking at his watch, he told Leo it was well after noon. "Whatever time it is, my father and brother aren't here. If you'd like to talk to them, then you'll have to come back. Sometime later in the day."

"Sure, but we're here to talk to you. It's about your father." He said that he didn't care so long as he wasn't dead. "He is, I'm afraid. This morning your time."

The man looked upset for all of a second. Then he looked around the dirty kitchen and invited them in. Bumping into the table, he not only knocked over the glasses there, but the empty pizza and chicken take out boxes as well. Leo hit several more things as he made his way to the living room.

The wheelchair Leo was in was one of the more expensive models. He wasn't getting around as well as Xander had thought he would, but then, he wasn't there for a critique on his driving skills. When the woman came from the back room with a maid's outfit on, Taylor snickered, and he just stared at her when she bent at the waist and showed off her naked ass.

"My sister." No one laughed, though they didn't believe Leo either. "She's been helping me with some of the physical therapy."

"Sure she has. And I'm his uncle's monkey." He started to correct Charles, but knew that he'd only make things worse. "She sure has a nice hiney, don't you think? I'd like a hiney like that. Sitting right over my face."

"Behave." Taylor laughed then when Leo asked him what was going on. "Never mind. Anyway, I wanted to tell you that your father was killed this morning. The bullet was intended for someone else, but he was—"

"Does that mean that someone else will have to pay for his funeral?" He sounded hopeful, and it made Xander sick to his stomach. "We don't have any money around here. I mean, I get a check once a month, but that mostly goes to my brother. He takes my checks."

"He does?" Leo nodded. "Well, that sucks. And I'm not sure who will be paying for it if anyone will. There was some talk that he might be put into one of the cemeteries closer to the church. They're free, with only a donation to—"

"I don't have a donation either." Sure, he didn't. Xander sat down and looked around the room. There were more electrical things in this one room than he had in his entire house. "People like to give me stuff. Me being in a wheelchair and all. How can I turn it down if it makes them feel better?"

"Perhaps you can sell some of it." He was shaking his head even before he finished speaking. Taylor got up and started to walk around. "You don't seem all that concerned about your dad. Don't you have any feelings that I can talk to you about?"

"You a counselor or something?" He said that he was, thanks to his brother. "Yeah? Well, I don't need your head fixing shit. My father just died."

The waterworks were next. Not any tears, though he wasn't sure what to call the dry sobs. When he was finished, or to him, appeared to be, he looked at what Taylor was staring at. A photo hanging on the brand-new fridge.

"That was taken of me when I was younger." Taylor said he didn't look much older now. "Good genes, I guess. Me and my dad, we like to travel when we have the money. It's been difficult lately, because of me not being able to get around as well."

"Really? I would have thought with the laws the way that they are, you'd have all sorts of places that you could go. And this is in Italy, if I don't miss my bet. That must have been expensive." Taylor handed Xander the picture. Flipping it over, he just had time to see the date, last month, before it was snatched from him.

"If you guys are done, you should go now. I have to grieve." Taylor nodded just as Charles disappeared again. "You two are annoying, if you ask me."

"Yes, we are. I didn't introduce us to you. You didn't seem to mind, but I'd like to do so now. My name is Xander Winchester. My wife is Addie." Leo didn't seem impressed. "This is my brother Gabe. He's a doctor. And Taylor is an FBI agent. Taylor, come say hello."

Taylor smiled and shifted into his cat as he approached the man. The big tiger laid his head on Leo's lap. When Leo screamed loudly but didn't move, Xander was sure that they'd made a mistake. Then Taylor put his massive paw on his leg and extended his claws.

The leap from chair to floor was quick. But what was funny was when he stood up, danced around the room, then jumped up on the table, knocking more things to the floor. Taylor must have been feeling playful, because when he stuck his nose in one of the containers and showed it to Leo, the man screamed over and over and wet his pants.

"Mother of Jehoshaphat get that thing out of here. Why the fuck would you bring a lion to my house in the first place?" Xander corrected him. "I don't really give a rat's two toots, get him the fuck out of my house. What the fucking hell

132

is wrong with you?"

"Nothing. With you either, it appears." When Taylor went to the other room, to change into the clothing that he'd tossed in the window of the bathroom earlier, Leo stayed on the table. "My brother is a doctor, I pointed that out to you. And he's working for the state. Not as an insurance person, though they'll take his word for this. You're not a nice guy, bilking the insurance company for all kinds of shit you didn't deserve."

"You can't prove any of this." Xander pointed at the camera on his chest. It didn't work, but Leo wouldn't know that. "Then it's a miracle. I've been cured. That big tiger, he cured me."

"No, I'm afraid that won't fly either." He asked Gabe why not. "Because had you been only just cured, then you'd still not have been able to walk. Your muscle tone would have been nonexistent, your bones would have been weak. Not to mention, that was an Olympic style leap you did there to get away from him. And we have it on good authority that you were having a nice fuck time with your sister there."

"No way." Gabe nodded and did the circle with his finger going in and out of it to demonstrate what he was talking about. "You seen us? Christ, man. How far will you go to make a man feel bad about a little lie?"

"Little lie? No way. You're going to jail for insurance fraud. And over a decade of getting benefits that were never meant for you. Not to mention, all these things that people sent you because you were hurt." Taylor shook his head as he returned to the room, finishing up his charges. "You have a long list of shit that you're going to go to jail for, for a very

133

long time. And the really sad part is, you did this to your brother. He didn't have any idea."

"He did too. He knew all along." Taylor just shook his head. "He did. It was all his idea. I wanted to walk around and stuff, but he said it would play better at his job if I just did this. Yes, it was all his idea."

"Even if he did know, we have enough on him right now to put him away for a long time. You too." When he was read his rights, Leo kept asking about his things. All the nice gifts that he'd been given over the years. "Those will be sold off in an auction or donated. The money will go to your victims."

He was screaming about his rights as a cripple—Leo's words, not Xander's—as he was taken to the police car. When the sister—her name was never given as she said it wasn't required by her—but when she found out that she wasn't going to get paid for her time, her fit was rivaled only by Leo's song and dance about his things.

"You did well in there." Xander thanked Taylor. "Have you thought about running for office? Columbus could use a guy like you. And it doesn't hurt that you have a wife that is as bad-assed as yours is."

"Nah, I'm writing, and it fills up a lot of my time. You should run." He shook his head. "Why not? I think your wife has the same qualifications. And you're going to be staying around here, right?"

"Her dad wants me to take over his leap. And it is around here, just outside of Columbus." He nodded and waited for the man to say he wanted to do it. "I don't, in the event you're asking. I don't want to be leap leader just yet."

"Have you told James?" He said that he was having

dinner with him tonight to talk it over. Then he asked if he'd go. "You might want to have an alternate plan if you tell him you're not going to take his job right now. Tell him...I know — tell him as police chief, you'd be better at the rules and laws of humans. Not that you're not already, but small towns, I've noticed, have a set of rules that don't apply to the bigger city ones. Not that they're against the law, just more laid back. That might be a better way to go with him."

"I'm telling you right now, Xander. If you run against me in this, I'm going to sock you right in the nose. You're good at this." He nodded, and Charles told him to tell him about the extra help he could give him. "You see ghosts?"

"No, just two. Well, one now. I have Charles with me all the time now. And then there is Asim that is a part of me, as well as Bug who lives on Addie. Oh, and it's Gabe that sees the ghosts, him and his wife Rayne. Rayne can even send them away when necessary. She's the death watcher. Caleb is the—"

"Enough." He smiled at his new friend. "Christ, I'm never going to be able to keep you all straight — you know that, don't you? What does your mom do? Or your father? I'm sure that they have some sort of power that makes it so you can't lie to them."

"Nah. But I'd not lie to my mom. She can see through you all the way to the back of your shirt. And my dad's power is his little off the cuff sayings. Mom can bake a pie out of anything and have you begging for more." They were both laughing as they went out to the car, where Gabe seemed to be having a conversation with himself. "He's got trouble. I don't know what is going on, but it can't be good."

135

"No, I can see that." When Gabe turned to look at him, he could see the horror on his face. "Come on, Xander, let's see what we can do to help him out."

"There is a body here." Nice way to start a conversation, he told his brother. "It's the mom. She's been here for a very long time, and is unaware of what is going on. She's been murdered most brutally. And is unaware of how she ended up here."

"What can we do to help?"

Xander was proud of Taylor. He didn't miss a beat in asking him what was needed rather than making fun or something about what Gabe could do. He was going to do well as the new police chief. As Gabe told him what needed to be done, he reached out to Addie, who was working on talking to Lyman. It had been a really shitty day for the Birdman family.

~*~

Lyman tried his best to absorb what was going on right now. Addie had been in his sights for so long, he couldn't equate her with the woman she was being right now, visiting him in the hospital. The woman was nice, talking to him about what had gone down today. And she was very nice in telling him that not only had his brother been arrested, but his father was dead. Lifting up his hand, she stopped talking.

"You're telling me that someone was hired to kill you and you believe it was my dad. Why would he care? I mean, you were on my work load, not his." She didn't tell him anything that he didn't already know. "Yes, he's an ass, but there has to be a reason that he'd kill you."

"Me and my partner. Jamie." He shook his head. There

136

was more, he just wasn't sure he wanted to hear it just yet. "Your father thought that Jamie was a male. And that killing us would get you fired. You were so jealous of us, me and this other man, supposedly, that you took your anger out on us and that was what would get you fired. You told him and your brother how you put out to have Boone killed. He talked to someone else about that, and was hired to find a killer to do the job for him."

"My dad works for someone else? That's not possible." But it might be, his mind screamed at him. He thought of the things that had just come into the house recently. "We have a new computer. A stereo system too. And then there is the new appliances, as well as the barn out back."

"Things paid for by someone wanting us dead. Did you know that Leo has been able to walk since he came home from the hospital? The wheelchair was necessary in the beginning, but after that, when the things and cards of sympathy came in, some with cash, they decided to cash in on it. There are other things too, welfare that your brother was receiving, that your father applied for. Things like rallies and fundraisers brought in more cash and gifts." It was too much. He wanted to cry. After all this time— "My partner just went to the house and your brother has been walked out of your home. On his own two feet."

"No, no. That can't be right. Leo was forever telling me how lucky I was that my mother hadn't killed him. That she'd been murdered, by my dad, because of…. Is he really dead?" She nodded at him. "And you're telling me that my brother is in jail, that he can walk?"

"Yes. He walked out of the house on his own." She sat

down then, her badge evident now that he knew to look for it. CIA. She was a sniper for the CIA. "Lyman, there was never going to be anything between us. I thought, even now, that telling you straight out was the best way to go."

"It wasn't you. Christ, I've made a mess of everything. While I was lying here before you came in, all I could think about was what my family was going to say to me. That I was never going to live this down." She nodded as if she understood. Which, he was pretty sure, she didn't. "My brother has been holding it over my head for decades that he was a cripple, that he deserved to be treated the way he was. I wonder what our dad would have said. Wait, he would have known. Christ, they took all those vacations together, and I was never able to go with them."

"Yes, that was the big thing that set them off. And the money in an offshore account. They're being paid by someone to keep an eye on you so that they could get information about jobs, people that you were or might be working with. Had you not had Boone killed, they would have. He was on their list too." Lyman nodded. "You're going to jail too, Lyman."

"I figured as much. Treason for one thing. Murder. Lying to a superior officer. That might not sound like much to you, but he was the president, and that is going to cost me." She didn't say anything, just stared at him. "When I go to prison, will I be alone then? I mean, as an FBI agent, I'm not going to be in the public, am I?"

"No, you'll be given a cell well away from the public population. Also, you'll have at least an hour a day out in the sunshine. Again, alone. Of course, there are things you could help us with, to maybe get you a few more perks should you want them. A desk, perhaps. Computer time to do what you want. I'm not saying that'll come true, but some things can happen." He asked her what they'd be. "Your mother. Do you know where she might be buried?"

"Behind the shed that's to the left of the house. I put flowers on it every year on her birthday." She told him she'd get someone on it. "There are others too. Not by my hand, but others. I can tell you where they're buried as well. One you're never going to find. My dad, and now I can assume my brother, put a man into a wood chipper once. Just after seeing that movie. Dad said it was messier than it showed in the television set. I should have said something, but to be honest with you, I was just barely hanging on to my job as it was."

"That isn't going to fly, and you know it, Lyman. You had a duty and you failed it." He nodded but said nothing. What could he say, anyway? There was nothing left for him to do other than to tell all. "Lyman, will you help us?"

"Yes. I cheated on my exams. And I didn't rape that woman, but they never believed me. Now, with all this, I know it was more than likely my brother, and since I never knew that he could do anything like that, I used him as my defense. The trouble was, he used me for his own." She told him he was being recorded again. Not that things mattered at the moment, but he told her his name, the rank that he'd been, and that he was doing this without payment of any kind, no promises had been made to him, and that he was doing this of his own free will. "My family had been after me for a long time to join the service. I have no idea why they thought I'd make a good soldier. But when they were hiring at the FBI office, I though why not? I never knew it was so difficult."

"You took the tests." That was all the prompting he was going to get, he supposed. But he told her again that he'd cheated on the tests. "Who helped you cheat?"

"My father. He did that. He wrote everything down on these little sheets of paper for me. I never thought he could spell that well. Do you suppose he had help as well? Anyway, water under the bridge, I suppose. I also did drugs, whenever I could, to get settled. My family again. I hate to keep blaming it all on them, but they were difficult to—" He thought of something then. "They made it so I had to live at home. Making it difficult for me to get a place of my own, as well as causing trouble with landlords. Every time I tried to move out, they'd reel me back in with one thing or another. Not always my brother, but that was a part of it. They wanted me there to...I have no idea why, but they wanted me there."

He was chained to the bed when they were finished. A guard, one of his own men, was put in the room with him. Suicide watch, they'd told the others, but he and the man with him knew what a total waste of dog shit he really was.

Lyman wasn't allowed a television. He was hoping, when they came in to take it out, that he might be able to get a glimpse of his brother walking on his own two feet. But it wasn't going to happen now. And when his guard told him that they'd found his mom, he decided that life, for him, was just too much to handle.

He did want to end his life. Today if he could manage it. To be so free of life's troubles would be wonderful, he thought. There wasn't really anything for him to look forward to, other than a few hours in the sunlight once he was put in prison. But there was not going to be enough for him to keep at, to keep his mind working all the time. Boredom wasn't something that he did well.

Looking around his room, he tried to think what he could use to off himself. There was nothing. The room's only chair had been taken by his guard. The table had long since been taken out. The television, as well as the knobs on the dresser, were gone. It occurred to him that there wasn't even a bathroom in this room, and he wondered about that. Not that he'd ask out loud, but he did have a thought or two about it.

For fun he thought of all the reasons there wasn't a bathroom. Well, the person in here couldn't walk. That opened the pain back up about how his family had duped him, and he thought of other reasons. Like the fact that the person in this room had been shot in the leg and he couldn't walk yet. Yes, that sounded better. He looked at his own shoulder as he sat there.

His father had done this. Had hired a person to fire into the group of people that he was near. Lyman wouldn't have been on his list to kill. No, he was some sort of moneymaker for him. Whatever he made, Lyman had never seen a penny of it.

He wondered what would make a person lie to his son about his brother. Lyman had no doubt that they both knew about it. And he thought of the things he'd thought about when he and Leo would take those trips. They never wanted him to go because if he did, then he'd be able to tell on them about Leo. Lyman didn't think that he would have told. But then, he never got the chance to prove himself to them.

141

"Why do I care?"

The guard said nothing as Lyman lay there. He'd more than likely been told to listen to his every word and then tell them of it later. Again, why did he care? As it was now, he was going to be spending a great deal of time behind bars. So lying there, he thought of things that he could tell Addie.

She'd been nice to him. Even, when he thought about it, in how she'd told him that she didn't want to see him. Up front and honest, just as she was telling him that he wasn't going to date her. Nor anything else. And she'd not done it so that he would be ridiculed in front of his colleagues either.

He also thought about all the things he'd done to his people. The ones that not just worked for him, but with him as well. Lyman had been a terrible person. Not even worthy of all the things he'd gotten with his job—the perks. Perks that he'd never used, but his father and brother had.

Today. It was going to be the first day of his life. He was not just going to be a better person, but a human being as well. Things were going to be different from now on. In his life, his mannerisms, as well as the way he did things. Prison, he knew, wasn't going to be good for him. But it might be better than he had it now. At least there, no one would be taking pot shots at him. Nor would he be hurting others. A sort of self-imposed better him.

Chapter 9

Xander watched Addie. One wrong move and the world could come tumbling down on not just him and her, but his entire family. Again, she was going over the plan. There wasn't any way that he'd be involved in this. He would surely become either a target or a hostage. Instead, he let her plan and plot while he made sure that she had all the supplies that she needed, as well as support.

"He'll want to know why I'm there." They'd gone over this before, several times, but Taylor was worried. And he didn't blame him. This was a big fucking deal. Right or wrong, no one was going to come out of this unscathed. "Tell me again what I need to say."

"Taylor, you can do this." Jamie hugged him to her as she laid her head on his shoulder. "You're going to do just fine. I know that. And you should too. Just act like this is a training mission, and it'll be easier for you to deal with."

He hugged her. The two of them had become a good set

of tigers. Mates that didn't walk all over each other, and had done a great job of supporting each other and boost each other up when they needed it. Wolves weren't even like that. They would support, but could bully you into doing the job. He looked over at Addie as she spoke to the man who was helping them. Ben had become a good friend as well.

"All right. I'm ready to go." Taylor kissed Jamie and then left. But he returned a second or two later, kissing Jamie again. Then he left for good. This was going to be hardest on him, he thought.

The plan, as small as it was, was going to net a great many people. Not just the one that Taylor was going after, but a long line of people, humans too, that had been fucking around with people's lives for a good long time. Xander looked over at Jamie and decided that this would make a good story someday. Just not yet.

Instead of waiting around with the rest of the people in the room, Xander went to his office. It had come a long way since he'd started this project. Now not only did he have a new computer, which he had needed since college, but he also had a fax machine—which surprised him with how much he'd used it—as well as a large copier.

Charles joined him a bit later, just as he was bringing up their second book together. "I saw my book. You put my name on it. Why on this God's good earth would you do something like that?"

"You helped me. And since the story is about you, I thought it would be a nice touch as co-author." He smiled at the man. "You know, I was also hoping that it would help me see if there was anyone out there that might know you. You said once that you fathered a child or two."

"Lies. I told them so often back in the day that I never really got the hang of telling the truth. I told you, for the first time in my whole durn life, the truth. Felt like I'd been awakened. You know what I mean?" He said that he did. "When I was a boy, there weren't no one around to gainsay me. Just a bunch of people that would rather hit me than to help me. I was starved most of the time. Then when I turned me sixteen, I joined the Army. Best thing I ever done did."

"At sixteen, you must have been about the youngest man there." Charles told him that he wasn't the youngest by far. There were some that were only about ten. "My goodness."

"Yeah. Some families, they got themselves too many mouths to feed or they just can't do it. Better than what some people did. They sold off their young'uns, and then when they got killed or something befell them, they said it was God's will. I think that God would have been happier had they just kept their kids with them. That's why you have them, ain't it?"

"I agree with you there. My mom and dad, they were broke. It wasn't until I was older that I realized just how broke we were. Mom would take in mending. Dad would plow other fields with his broken-down tractor for extra. All our gifts were handmade, and we were lucky to have gotten them."

He thought about his brother Owen's friend, Clay. How they'd been so poor and the mother had suffered from depression and killed them all, including herself. He remembered what his brother had told him about the confrontation between mother and son. And with her husband too. It was very painful. And Clay hadn't forgiven her. Xander wasn't sure that he would have been able to either.

They talked well into two hours before things were starting to work on the other end. He would hate to be Taylor right now, and the worse part was, he was pretty sure that Taylor hated being Taylor too. When Addie entered his office, he wasn't sure if he should run or go to her.

"He's there." Nodding, Xander asked if he should do something. "Yes. Hold me. This is something that I never in all my life thought would come to pass. And you know as well as I do what it took for Jamie to do this. For her own leap."

"You told me that she'd been doing it for a long time. Looking into the leap." Addie nodded as she sat across from him. "I thought you wanted me to hold you."

"I do. Actually, I want more than that. But if this thing goes where I think it will, then having you hold me won't get me anywhere near where we are now." He wasn't entirely sure what that meant so asked. "If we go to bed and have screaming sex — because, my dear, I'm going to make you scream — then nothing will be done when it needs to be done down here."

"I guess so. But it would be fun." She snorted at him. "You're so mean to me. I don't think you appreciate me as much as you should."

"You should appreciate that I don't pull my gun out and shoot you on a daily basis." He didn't laugh. Honestly, he wasn't sure that she wouldn't do just that. "I'm joking, Xander. Why are you so tense all the time lately?"

It was on the tip of his tongue to tell her it was her fault, but he knew that it wasn't. Tense? Yes, he supposed he was. He had a movie deal going down. He had a new mate. There were issues with the president. They had just arrested an FBI agent and his brother. Who, he thought, was the worst kind of criminal — he'd been sucking the system dry. And on top of all that, he had magic.

The magic part wasn't that big of a deal. Yes, he had a lot of it, most of which he didn't use all that much. The tats didn't bother him either. He had them, but they didn't interfere with his work. It was, he figured, all of it at once.

"What are you thinking about so hard?" Xander told Addie, all of it. "You do know that there is nothing really to what you're thinking about. I mean, it's all just stuff. When I was first out in the world, after spending years, decades, working on my craft to protect others, I was terrified. I knew that I'd been created to kill. Well, not just kill, but to help them. But it got to the point that I was doing more of the work than them doing it. Like organizing things. Getting people to train for the upcoming whatever. Mostly, the kings that I would go to work for, they'd be sitting on their asses and waiting for me to slay their enemies without them having to even show up. That didn't sit well with me."

"What did you end up doing?" She told him that she'd walked away when the army for the other side came calling. "I bet that went over well."

"Not so much." They both laughed. "I bet you're wondering what this has to do with your being overwhelmed. It does and it doesn't. What it does is, hopefully, show you that you're not alone. And that you don't wait around for things to go ass up or not. You do something about it."

147

"And the does not part of it?" She came and sat on his lap, holding him to her as she laid her forehead to his. "This is very nice, but not answering my question."

"You're always going to have me here for you. Not just at your side, but wherever you need me. Back, front, sides, I don't care, I have you. And when the roles are reversed, then I know that you're going to be there for me as well. Anywhere and anytime that I need you." He kissed her, giving her all that he had. "Xander, had you been with me all my life, I would have been a much better person, I think."

"I think that you're perfect." Standing up, he sat her on the desk and took a step or two back. "But I can hear my family and they need us. Taylor is doing well, but it's time you left for him."

Another kiss and she left him. The great falcon disappeared from the open window a few seconds later. Xander made his way to the living room—Taylor Central, it was called. Just as he entered the room, he saw Asim move and become a part of his body. Since Bug was missing, he assumed that he was with Addie. This was about to go bad or well, depending on which side you were on.

~*~

Addie made herself very small as she entered the large room. It was lavish, the room of the leap, and she had a thought that few entered this room. And those that did wondered why he had gold plated goblets on a shelf, or the head of a large lion.

That startled her the most. A lion's head? He was a tiger, yes, but to have a lion on the wall meant all sorts of things to her. Moving along the baseboards, she was quiet...well,

148

she was as quiet as the mouse that she was. The men were only talking, and she decided to wait for the signal before she took over. If she had to. Taylor seemed to have things under control, for now.

"I've come to do this formally." James nodded. "The hand of your daughter is very important to me, and I want us to be friends as well."

"I'd like that. I would." James asked Taylor to have a seat. "I don't usually see people in this office. It's more formal than the other one. Things that I've collected over the years. And if, someday, you decide to take over for me, you'll be able to have this as your office as well."

"What about the lion there? That looks out of place, don't you think?" Taylor laughed, and even from where she was, it didn't sound forced or strained. "I mean, you being a cat and all. I never thought that I'd see that on a wall of a leap leader."

"You'd be surprised, I think, of all the things one can do and places one can go when a leap leader like me." Taylor asked him what he meant. "A man of means. A leader of all this. Did you know that I have over one thousand people under me? And, for the most part, I think they love me. I keep them safe."

"I've been walking around the area. There are some that grumble." He asked him why he'd listen to them. "Well, Jamie and I, we're trying to figure out where we're going to stay when we get married."

"You'll stay here." Taylor laughed. "This is not a joke, young man. You'll stay here. And you can work for the government—in fact, I would encourage it. But you're not leaving my leap. You can, I suppose, but Jamie isn't going with you."

"Wouldn't that be for her to decide?" James shook his head, then laughed. "I don't know what you'd think was funny. I believe you just threatened me."

"Oh, you have that all wrong, young man." She was sort of relieved by that. "I actually was threatening you. If you leave here, you're not taking my daughter. I have plans for her. And if you try to take her, I'll kill you. No ifs, ands, or buts about that. You'll be as dead as anyone else that crosses me. What I'd do, if I were you, is just keep my mouth shut and do as you're told."

"And what would that be?" James laughed, but it sounded angry to her. "You want something from me, right? This coming here to ask you for her hand, it was just a ruse."

"Of course it is." James leaned back in his chair and pulled out a gun. He didn't lay it on the desk as she assumed he would, but held it up so that Taylor could see it. "You talk to my daughter and I'll blow that fucking head of yours off. Now."

"What do you want from me, James? I'm assuming you have something in mind." He nodded. Taylor was getting angry himself. "I'm not going to be your lapdog or cat. Tell me straight up or I'll walk now."

"I have your mother." That startled her. She knew that Taylor had a mom, but not that she'd be a pawn in all this. "And you'll do what I tell you, when I tell you, or she's as dead as that father of yours."

"My father isn't dead." James said that he was now. "Why would you do that? Why would you kill my dad? He was nothing to you."

150

"Because he was everything to you. This is the way it's going to work. When I ask you for information, you're going to get it for me. Jamie does it now, but in a less helpful kind of way. She tells her dear daddy everything—and I mean every little thing—that is going on. The man that shot and killed my other man, Finch, he's gone now, and I'll need a replacement for him. You'll do just fine."

"And if I don't want to?" The bullet sound echoed in the room as Taylor cried out. He was shot in the leg and would heal from it, but it had to be painful. But until he said the right phrase, she waited on him. "You plan to shoot me until I agree? You've already taken my father away from me, what else will you do? And why?"

"I've grown accustomed to having all that I want. And you'd be surprised at how much money people pay to have more information than they can use. For instance, did you know that other countries would like the name of that friend of yours? Addie Dyer is on just about everyone's list of known hitmen." Taylor said nothing as the second shot was fired. "You'll get her, and you'll do it without causing me any trouble."

"No, I won't." She waited; now was the time, she wanted to scream at him. But Taylor only sat there, his body hard with anger and pain. "I won't give her up any more than I'd work for you. You're a monster."

Say it, her mind screamed. And just as she was ready to shift and help him anyway, she felt the touch of Xander. He was calm, but also fearful for his friend.

He's in pain, but he also knows that the silver in the bullets won't hurt him. Make him sick, yes, but not hurt him too much.

151

And, so you know, Ben is listening in on your mic. She had the mic on her person, not on Taylor. She had been terrified that he'd be searched. *Just go with the plan. So far, all we have is him shooting Taylor. Nothing much more than speculation.*

Taylor was moaning, but James was laughing. Things were going to go bad for both men if they didn't get the information that they wanted. Like who did he report to, and why? There were other things too, material on who he gave what information to, but she could wait on that for now. One touch and she'd have it. But now, they needed a big reason to arrest and detain him.

"When my daughter first got into the service, I thought that she was turning butch on me. Her mother did. Decided that she liked women a hell of a lot better than she did me. Well, nipped that in the bud, didn't I? Her and that lover of hers will never be found." James laughed again. "Same with your father, but that's for another time. Say you'll work for me and I'll call someone to remove the bullets. Come on now, you can do it."

"I'm not going to say a word until you tell me exactly what it is you think I'm going to be doing for you." James told Taylor that he loved his spunk. "Yes, so the fuck what. What do you want?"

"You'll wed and bed my daughter as soon as possible. Then there will be no turning back from what I want you to do. After that, you'll continue working for that fucker of a president, and make sure that I get all the information you give to him." James leaned back in his chair again. "I know that you're not telling my lovely daughter what is going on. You have no wire on you to record this, and no one in their right mind will believe what you tell them about this meeting. If they do, then they'll be as dead as you will be if you try anything stupid. I'm going to be your father-in-law, dick weed, and the sooner you remember that, the better off you might be."

"And children—I suppose you want me to raise them in the same way you're treating me. A criminal." James laughed. "What do you think that Jamie would do if she found out what a monster you are?"

"Monster? I suppose I am. Not that I care what you think, but she'll never believe you. Once you start talking, it'll be the last words you utter. I'll have you dead so quickly that you'll not ever see it coming." Taylor said he had big words. "You think? Well, let me tell you about some of my other accomplishments. I have so many people working for me at the moment, that fucker in the White House can't take a shit without me knowing all there is to know about it. I know when he comes in his wife, when they have people over. What the meal was. Even who ate what from their plate. I'm telling you, Taylor, you just don't want to fuck around with me."

Addie thought about what he was saying. Either someone on the staff was helping him or the wife was. And she'd bet on the wife. Addie didn't know why, but she'd never liked the woman.

You deal with this and I'll deal with my home life. She said yes, sir before she remembered that Ben was listening too. *I'm sure you know as well as I that no one will ever miss her. And she won't just leave either. She'll be gone.*

You knew. He said that he'd already figured it out a week ago. *I'm sorry sir. Is she under some kind of blackmail or is she just doing it? Whatever the reason, I'll help you handle this.*

Yes, I had hoped that you would. In the meantime, I want you to listen to young Taylor. I like him, and I don't want to see him hurt too much more. Also, before this is done and I have to move back to the House, I want to exchange blood with all of you. Including Taylor.

Yes. All right, but that would be up to him. He said for her to make it happen. *Yeah, sure. Have you met him? He's not exactly the push over type. But I will try.*

She realized that he hadn't answered her, but was all right with that. He was a good man, someone that she'd grown to respect. This was as much a blow to him as it would be to the world if they ever found out about it.

When James stood up, she realized that she might have missed something. Conferring with Bug, he said that things were all right, but she heard the door opening and closing and knew that this could not be good. When Jamie entered the room with them, she knew that it had gone from shit to majorly fucked up.

"Hello Dad. I knew you were here with my— What happened here? Dad?" He told Jamie that Taylor had staggered in like this. "Are you kidding me? Why haven't you called an ambulance?"

She pulled out her cell phone and was ready to dial when it was jerked away from her. Her father, pointing the gun at her, told her to sit too. Jamie knew what was going on, but she was playing right into his hands. For now, Addie thought.

"Dad, what's going on? I though you and Taylor were going to talk." The gun wavered a little but didn't lower. "Dad?"

"Shut up." Addie heard her teeth slam shut, but it wasn't the end of this. James began walking around the room. "Why did you have to come here? Damn it, Jamie, don't you ever listen to what you're told?"

"Rarely. What's the meaning of this? Why is Taylor shot?" James told her that he'd done it. "No, I won't believe that. Why have you shot him?"

"He's trying to kill me. He was trying to kill me." Jamie looked at Taylor, then back at her father without saying a word. "You don't believe me? Ask him. He drew out his own weapon and shot at me. Had I not been quick on my feet, he would have killed me."

"I don't see any bullet holes except the ones in him. What did you do, Dad?" He laughed bitterly. "You're not making any sense. He came here to talk to you about marrying me. And since I have the patience of a bug, I couldn't wait."

"I thought I could make the two of you heel, but I can see that you're much too much like your mother. Damn it all to fuck and back, Jamie, why didn't you just mind me and stay away?" She asked him if he had planned to kill her mate. "Yes, if it came to that. But now? Well, I'm not sure that I won't have to kill you both. Damn it."

"What's this about, Dad? Why have you shot Taylor? He's my mate. You know what happened to you when Mom left." He laughed. Taylor told her what had happened. "You killed my mom? You actually killed my mom? Why? What had she ever done to you?"

"She was a gay fucking woman." Jamie looked right at her, but didn't speak as her father continued. "She found herself having a taste for pussy, and I could not stand that.

155

What was I to do? Let her have her fun? Maybe I would have if they had let me have fun too. But no, they were prudes about that. They'd eat each other out, but they wouldn't let me fuck them while they did it. So I murdered them both."

"You're insane." James said that he wasn't, but was a man who got what he wanted. And he wanted her to shut the fuck up and listen to his plan. "No, I don't think so. Taylor and I are leaving this room this minute."

The signal was there, so Addie simply made herself whole and the fighting engine that she'd been created to be. At about the time that James realized she was in the room, he was dead—he'd just not fallen to the floor yet.

Chapter 10

Xander watched her. There wasn't any way that he could touch her skin right now without becoming covered in blood like she was. Besides, he thought, the powers that were there, all G-men he'd come to hate, had been close enough to her that he thought they'd shoot first.

When she'd killed James it had been messy, and not nearly as quick as she'd wanted it to be. The man had fought back, but it was lost even before it began. She called out every name that he'd harmed, the people that he'd killed, the children that were lost to those that had been bombed because of the information that he'd sold to their foreign enemies. Addie — his Addie — had been judge, jury, and executioner.

Now she was with the people that wanted things answered. Most she just ignored, as seemed to be her way, and the others, she would tell them very little. Answering the questions that were put to her, he noticed something else about her.

She wasn't just calm, but sort of bored looking. The expression on her face, the one that she was showing the public, was belying the turmoil that she was feeling inside. He wasn't in any doubt that she had hated killing the man. He'd been someone that she knew well and hadn't expected this from him.

Ben came to stand beside him as he waited. "In one week, she's going to come to me. When she does, I would like it if you came with her. My wife, you see. She needs to be taken care of. There is no telling who else she works for." He only nodded. "Xander, I have a favor to ask of you. One that I think you're going to turn me down on, but I'm going to ask all the same."

"I'm not in the mood for twenty questions. Just ask." Ben laughed, and he smiled. "You're a bastard, did you know that?"

"I have been called worse, I hate to say. My favor—I'd like for the two of you to go on a long vacation. One that takes you out of the country for a while." He asked who they were going to kill while gone. "Such a cynic, aren't you? But yes, I have someone that needs to be taken care of."

"When she was working for you, or whatever this relationship is called, why didn't you have her kill off some of the bigger names? Boone didn't seem all that bad, not like a lot of them I've read about. I mean, besides murder and mayhem, what did he do that countless others haven't?"

"I can't tell you right now. When I get you on the same page as Addie, and that'll be soon, I can tell you just about anything you want." He looked at the president. "I can have people killed, Xander, and not think a thing of it. So long as the nation as a whole isn't harmed. But if you get hurt because of the information that I could share with you, then I'd never be able to live with myself."

"Addie is all I have ever wanted in a mate. More than I ever dreamed I'd have since I thought that you only got one chance in this life for a mate." Ben told him he was sorry. "I'm not. Had I been mated to this other person, someone that I didn't know, then there is no telling what would have happened to me. Or to Addie and you, for that matter. I'm sorry that she died, don't get me wrong, but I'm thrilled to no end that I have Addie in my life."

"I'm glad to hear that. Also, there is one more thing. As a government employee, you'll get all the benefits afforded to you. Perks that you won't believe." He nodded. "Don't you care about that?"

"I have a book coming out in a few days. A movie deal too. Right now, I'm so fucking overwhelmed by just that, that having the president tell me I have perks isn't even a blip on my radar."

Ben was still laughing when he left him standing there. Xander watched them take the body out of the house and the people straining to take pictures. He knew that no one would get a picture of him, nor of Addie or the other two. The ghosts, apparently, were working to keep those all blurred. He wondered if on camera he'd look like one of those carnival mirror reflections. It was the strangest thought that he'd ever had go through his head.

Addie had killed James. It hadn't been pretty, but neither was it quick. After Taylor and Jamie left, Addie had pulled out blades from her body and cut him up, and with each cut to his body, blood and other fluids sprayed over the room and her. She had been merciless in her killing him. Addie did it for all the people that he'd killed, simply because of what he'd done with information that wasn't his to give out.

The body had been put in pieces in the big bag. He knew this because he'd been in the room, the way it looked when things had gone down. The moment that Addie had risen from the floor as a tiny mouse, Asim had used his eyes so that he could watch his mate in action. Because no matter how he looked at it, Bug was his mate as much as Addie was, and the same was true for him and Asim.

She had toyed with James. Cutting him on the knees first—the same places that he'd shot Taylor. Then she'd sliced his belly open. Watching the man try to hold onto his guts was both satisfying as well as disgusting. Addie cut him over and over.

When she swung the same blades that were at his arms now, he didn't know what to think. She did it with style, precision, as well as deadly accuracy. When James's throat was cut, the blood pouring from his throat, Asim had stood over him and pissed on the open wound. James was long dead before he even felt the heat of it.

She had stood there, covered in blood, her chin dripping with the residue of it. When she turned and looked at Asim, he shivered once but didn't move. Honestly, he wasn't sure if it had been him or the great wolf. Then when Addie dropped to her knees, he was able to come into the room with her and touch her.

Her skin was hot, like she'd burned a great deal of energy and it was coming out of her. The blood smelled warm, fresh even. The man had spilled more than his guts—there was brain matter there too. And when she begged him to hold her, it was all he could do to shift and do just that. In moments, he held his one and only true love in his arms.

The police and the SWAT team arrived later. Xander was already out of the house, his body no longer covered in blood. When she had been asked about the smears of blood on her, she told them to fuck off. Best explanation he could have heard from her.

The SWAT team had said it was a good thing she was there to find James's body. A bomb had been set to go off sooner rather than later. But who had planted it and had killed Mr. Riddell, no one would ever know, never look for. His death would be mourned for months, they told her. It was the best plan, Xander thought, to rid the house of all the blood and other things that had been taken out before the people, spectators, had arrived.

It was a lie, of course. She'd murdered him. No, not murdered—she'd done her duty to the country and had killed a bad man. Addie had told him that when they'd been together. It wasn't murder, but her job. And today, with this man, she had enjoyed herself. When they seemed to be finished with her, she stepped into a tent and stripped off. The blood could be seen circling the small plastic tub from several feet away.

Finished with them all, she came to him again. Xander held her, her body shaking with spent magic. When a large glass of juice was handed to her, she drank it down, along with the gallon jug that she'd been handed as well. He would have to remember that from now on. To have plenty of it at the house when she came home.

"I want to go home." Xander said he'd like that as well. Penny, he told her, was waiting up for them. "Good. We should pick up some pizzas, have some soda, and make a night of it. She should be able to miss school tomorrow. Mommy here is exhausted."

Xander loved the way she said that. Also the way that she leaned on his shoulder. It wasn't enough, not really, but for now it would do. The ride home from Columbus in one of the perks in the form of a helicopter was punctuated with calls from his family, and also the president. As soon as she ended that call, she took the phone and broke it in half and tossed it out the window. Enough was enough, she told him.

Penny was indeed waiting for them. Not only was she in her jammies and wide awake, but she'd made them a sign, one that Xander knew they'd treasure forever. "Welcome back, Mom and Dad." It was more than he'd ever thought he'd have, and it was all right here in this house. A house that was finally a home.

~*~

Tyler hung up the phone and sat down. He wasn't sure whether for some reason Mr. Cartwright had somehow cursed him with these houses. All he did was travel to see to them. He was going to have to do something soon or he was going to have to sell them all to have some peace. His dad had suggested that he hire someone to go to them. That sounded to him like a great idea.

"Sir are you leaving again?" His cook—and the man who was fast becoming his right-hand man—Lloyd, smiled at him. "I can see by the look on your face that you are, and you're not happy about it."

"You'd think a man that was worth millions and has twenty-seven houses all around the world would be happy to go to France, but I just want to stay home. To hang out with my family. To be here." Lloyd said that he might know someone that could help him out. "Oh yeah? I'll hire them, sight unseen."

"She's a bit unorthodox. Has a nasty temper. The reason I know this is because I just got off the phone with her mother. They don't see that they're a great deal alike, and they butt heads all the time."

"Human?" He said that they were. "And it's just the two of them? No lurking children? No dogs that I have to vie for attention from?"

"No sir." He laughed. "There is a younger sister, Jazzie. She has a little boy. Poor thing, her husband died the day that she gave birth. A car accident. Took his life and that of another woman. And it was another woman, if you understand." He said that he did. "She doesn't come around as much as the other two would like, but she's still mourning, I think. Not for him, I don't believe, but— Sorry. I do so love that little girl."

"But the other one, you think that she'd do the job? And do it well?" He said that she was a real estate agent and also turned rentals. He asked her name. "Lavender—Laveen is what she goes by. Laveen Richardson. She's a beauty, sir. And a nut crusher, her mom said. But she will do the job and do it very well."

"Good. Ask her to.... You know what? Tell her to please come here and we'll go over whatever she needs to know. Christ. This is going to save me so much time. I know that I should have done this before, but this is just something that I thought I'd want to do. Understand?"

"I do sir, I really do. But as you said, you can't be running all over the place when it only needs to have — what is it that needs to be fixed this time?" He told him. "And they could not find someone there to change a light bulb on their own? I should like to fire that staff, sir. I think that would be the first thing I did."

"They're afraid of me." Lloyd snorted. "Laugh if you want, but they're afraid of me. I might have lost my temper a few weeks ago when I was there when I was going over receipts. They had replaced all the plumbing in the entire house. Now that doesn't sound like a bad thing, but it had only been redone six months ago. By their relative. It had to be replaced this time because of his spotty workmanship."

"You should have fired the lot of them." He had an idea, a big one, but it must have shown on his face. "Oh no. Whatever you're thinking, you just get it out of your head right now. What is it you're thinking?"

"I was thinking that you should go to France with this lady and see what I've been dealing with. Then fire them all. You could have a staff there, maybe someone from here, in charge that would keep the place running and up to par. It's a beautiful home. And like the rest of my homes, there is a staff quarters that has access to all sorts of perks." He asked what sort of perks. "A wine cellar. A grape arbor that has its own winery. There is a pool that someone could use."

"My daughter." Tyler didn't even know he had a daughter and told him that. "She's been looking for work here. Ashleigh has a business management degree, speaks several languages, and before you ask me why she's not working, downsizing. She was in upper management at the airport in town, and they let people go to save the company."

"All right. See if she wants to do it. Why didn't you help me before?" He grinned. "You wanted me to see if I could do it?"

"Oh, I knew you could do it, sir. It's just that you had to figure out for yourself that you needed some help. And you do. Very much so." He nodded and felt better already. "Ashleigh said that she'd take the job, and she'll travel with Laveen to get things settled there. If you don't mind, sir, I believe that Laveen's mother will want to travel with her. A free vacation, I'm thinking."

"Will that be trouble, you think?" Lloyd said that he didn't anticipate anything like that. They argued, but they were loyal to each other. All three of them. "All right. See if Jazzie would like to travel with them too. Maybe she wants to get away."

"Sir, that is asking for trouble. As I said, they are a good family, but the younger one, Jazzie, she hasn't been one that they get along with well." He nodded. "Perhaps she can go to another home that you have—one that is giving you trouble as well?"

"I'll think on which one is giving me the most trouble." Tyler felt like a new man. His homes were going to be taken care of. "If they need anything, like spending money, see that they have it in the form of credit cards, Lloyd. And they must keep the receipts for me."

After Lloyd went to make the calls, Tyler sat down at his desk. This was what he should have been doing all along, getting others to do the job. Calling his attorney, Wendell Forthright, he told him what he'd done and asked what he needed to get them employed.

"I hate to say this, Tyler, but it's about time." Thanking him, he told him the names of the people that he was going to interview. "I know Laveen. She was a hell of a real estate agent. Sold me my house. Also, she can do just about everything you need her to do. The only problem I foresee is that she's sort of a ball buster. What you need, but I'm fearful of the two of you clashing."

"So long as I don't have to do this, I can avoid her." He wondered, briefly, if she was his mate, then dismissed it. If he avoided her at all costs, then he was going to be fine. "Call her and get her started. I'm sold on her doing the job. And set it up so that Ashleigh, Lloyd's daughter, is going to go with her to run the place, and Laveen's mom—her name is Gardenia, I think—will be going as well. Get them set up with money, making sure they have the receipts as well as whatever else they might need."

When he hung up, Tyler felt great. He was going to go on a run when the phone rang. Telling Lloyd that he wasn't in, he left the house for the first run that he'd had in ages where he wasn't either pressed for time or something had pissed him off and he was running it off.

What are your plans for the day? He thought of his dad and having a big dinner with him. Asking him if he could work him into his schedule, Dad laughed.

I was thinking that too. But you've been so busy lately, that I ain't seen hide nor hair of you.

I just hired some people to work for me. Dad said the same

166

thing that Wendell had. *Yeah, I think I was trying to do it all by myself because it was left to me by a good friend. Sort of like I didn't want to mess it up.*

He'd have known that about you too. But this here dinner, you thinking we can ask the others to come along too? The boys, I mean. I wanna get your momma a big gift, and I need some help with that. I ain't never had the money to get her something pretty and expensive before, and I have my mind on a couple of things.

The dinner was planned, and he didn't think that he was going to take his cell phone. By the time they were ordering, Tyler figured, then the women would be in the house and have things all set up. Just the way he wanted. And Wendell was going as well, to set up accounts for the house sitters, as well as for his new real estate agent. Things might not be perfect, but at least he'd have someone else to help out. He just hoped he hadn't just hired his mate, that was all.

He didn't mind having a mate, but he was unsettled. Not that he was a party guy. He'd never been that. But he liked things to be normal...whatever the fuck that meant. As he got dressed, Dad wanting them to wear suits for a change, he thought of his mom's gift that he'd gotten for her.

Owen had given him six of the gems. Having them made into a bracelet for her, one for each of her sons, had been brilliant, he'd thought. Then Caleb decided that she needed something for the wives of them. That had become a bigger project, mostly because they weren't all there yet.

Xander was working on one for grandchildren. It was going to have a smaller gem, his idea, that was carried in a small pair of booties, with the date and year of birth and the name of the child on them. He thought it was going to be too heavy with all that, but Xander was excited for it.

Dad had been a little harder to choose for. He wasn't anyone that collected things. Like most fathers he knew, Dad didn't wear ties, and he didn't own any kind of pipes or stuff like that. Nor did he drink coffee or even hot tea. If he didn't need it, Dad didn't have it.

Buying him the big television had been a blast for them. The sixty-five-inch sucker was going to be epic when they watched games at home, and he thought that they might be spending more time there too. He looked over at himself when he'd fucked with his tie too much.

"A mate would have had this done by now." He wasn't sure why that thought popped into his head, but he smiled at himself. "You're an idiot if you only want a wife so that she can fix your tie for you."

Not in the habit of talking to himself, he left his room and headed downstairs. The dinner was going to be fun, and he wasn't going to worry about houses nor tenants. Not tonight.

Their favorite restaurant wasn't one that someone would think of as high class. The food was great, steaks cooked outside on a grill year-round. There was the best bread, too, to go with every meal, as well as corn bread if you got soup, and hard crackers for the salad. Tyler loved this place.

"I helped them out in this here place a couple of weeks ago." He asked his dad, the two of them being the first to arrive, what had happened. "Nothing bad. They needed a bigger grill and the salad thingy, not sure what they called it, pooped out. I guess they lost some food in it, and the insurance wouldn't cover that and a new machine."

"They need a new insurance company." He said that he'd

168

told them the same thing. "And what do you get in return for your investment? I mean, you did go to Wendell, right?"

"I did. But he wanted some kind of contract and all that. He changed his mind sure enough when I told him that I'd known old Banger for a long time and we had us an understanding." They did too. Tyler remembered it as well. "Tyler, what do you think about just putting together some of our money and helping out? I wanted to do that before, but we sort of got ourselves side tracked on things."

"I've been helping too, though not investing. I don't need a return." He said that he didn't either. "Well, what I've done is put out an application and ask people how much they need, what they need it for, and how they plan to pay it back. Not to me, but to the fund. That way, there is always money in the pot. And also, they have to hire one person who needs a job. Hopefully that's working out—I never heard."

"You know, I sure do like that. How is that going?" He told him that he'd helped nine people so far. "I'm betting it was Mrs. Quarter, ain't it?" He nodded.

"She only needed a new lawn mower. And when she got it, she hired a boy whose parents are struggling to come by and mow her yard for her. And the fund pays that too. It doesn't for everyone, but Mrs. Quarter, she doesn't have a lot anyway."

They talked about other shops that were having a hard time. People that needed a new roof, as well as some other things. The Sheppards needed a new furnace that Tyler was helping with. When the rest of them were there and seated, the talk continued about the town.

"I think that we should go out and stretch our muscles

169

and help that way too." Dominic asked what he meant. "Well, it won't hurt us none to go out and put a few nails to the wood, now would it? We can mow grass and trim with the best of them. I was thinking of coming up with a yard crew anyway, to take care of the landscaping stuff around the plants I have now. Mr. Cartwright, he kept them looking good, remember?"

"Yes, I do. Even though we had no idea that he owned them, he sure did have nice businesses." Tyler thought about the homes that he had and the one that he lived in now. "I don't think he ever had anyone doing the work on his house until we started helping him. I mean, he could have, I guess, but he held off for us. I miss that old man every day."

"Me too." Dad brought out his hankie and wiped at his nose. "I've been thinking of getting your momma a pretty weddin' band and a diamond. Then having us get ourselves hitched all over again. We was married on Christmas Eve, you know."

They did. And they all loved the idea. To see his parents all gussied up, as he called it, would be great. And they started planning things to go with it. They were going to take a long cruise in the new year, and the boys were going to pay for it. Tyler was excited to see Mom's face when she got their gifts to her and dad.

Chapter 11

Clare wasn't sure what she was doing here. Her parents had asked to see her and she had stupidly said yes. And the attorney said that he'd make it so that she could see them both at the same time, rather than having to be there twice as long. Besides, Clare had so much work lined up for the spring and after that — she was making her own cash now.

"Mrs. Winchester? They're ready to see you now. They told you the rules, didn't they, when you got here?" She nodded and repeated them back to him. "Good job. And I'm glad that you didn't bring them any treats. They'd just lose them again. They've not been model inmates."

"They were never model parents either. Thank you." He nodded, then hesitated a moment, and she was afraid of what he might be going to tell her. "They don't want to see me now?"

"Oh, yes ma'am, they do. But they have it in their head that you and your brother owe them something. And that you should be getting them out somehow. They know that you're married to a Winchester, and they're a big name around here. Not just because they got money now, but because—well, they're the Winchesters." She'd heard that before, that the Winchesters hadn't changed much, other than their addresses, when it came to helping out their town. "You don't let them bully you. That baby you're carrying, it's their grandchild, and you show her how it's done when it comes to them."

"I will. Thank you." The cookies that she'd brought were no longer something she wanted to give them. "Here, you take these and pass them around. I brought them as sort of a peace offering, but you're right, I didn't put them here."

Her mom looked like someone had beaten her recently. Dad didn't look all that much better. Being non-model inmates was getting them into trouble. But it wasn't her concern, she was going to keep telling herself. She was glad now that Conrad hadn't come with her.

Not that he wanted to. He told her that he had a job now and he didn't want to miss work. And the pay was giving him such a boost too. Conrad had a home of his own, with a live-in person. A new bicycle, as well as a studio that he used nearly every day. Plus a new camera that he was having fun taking pictures with. Her brother had grown up a great deal lately.

Sitting down, she asked them what they wanted.

"What a way to speak to us. I'm sure you think you're being cute, talking to me like that. But I am your dad, Clare, and I won't stand for it. Now, what are you doing to get us out of here? We've more than paid our debt to society." Her dad reached for Mom's hand when he finished, but was told no touching. "I hate that rule. I miss you, Ava."

"And I miss you too. They won't let me have a doctor come in here either. Just look at my face, Con. How am I supposed to go out in public looking like this?" He told her that she needed some more treatments. "Can I get them when I get out? I've not spent any time with my body in so long, I think I'm falling apart."

"And how do you suppose you did that?" They both looked at her as if they'd forgotten that she was still there. "You aren't getting out of here. Not any time soon, anyway. If you live long enough, you'll be about ninety-five or so when you're released."

"No, that won't work for us. We've plans, you see. That brother of yours, he needs to come here so that people can see that we have a retarded son so we can get out of here. Who is taking care of him, anyway? Are they getting paid? I could use that money." She said that he was doing just fine. "Yes, so you say. But he's a retard, Clare, not some normal person."

"He's not a retard, you bitch." Letting out a long breath, she stared at her mother again. "He's not a retard, Mother, he's normal. Conrad has his own home, a credit card. He even has a job that he loves."

"What the fudge does he have a job doing? Separating cans? Does he do sheets? Those are retard jobs." She asked her dad as politely as she could not to call him that. "But he is, Clare. Everyone knows that but you. It matters little. As his parents, I want you to have his money transferred to us. We have an account here that we're going to have to pay off before we leave here."

"Why do you think you're ever going to get out of here? Not to mention seeing Conrad or me. You're not, in case

173

you're wondering. I have a husband now, a baby coming too. A little—" She looked at their faces. "You're not happy about me having a baby?"

"Gracious no. Oh my God, Clare, how could you do that to us? We don't want to be grandparents until we're old. Probably not even then. A grandchild? That kind of thing will make us sound old. And we're not. Get rid of it. I demand that you do." Clare stared at her mom and then at her dad as he agreed, nodding vigorously about her aborting her child. "Well? What is it you need now? We want you to do those things and then get us out of here. We know you have money now. And so does Conrad, you told me. That should be plenty enough to have my face fixed, don't you think?"

"I'm a billionaire." She took great satisfaction in saying that to them. "My husband inherited a great deal of money recently, and we've been investing well and getting a good return on it. All my brothers-in-law are rich too."

"Well, that makes things much easier. We'll need you to— Where are you going?" Home, she told him. "Home? But we're not finished here, Clare. Sit down and listen to what we need for you to do. It's the least you can do for us."

"No." She did sit down, and saw the satisfied look on her dad's face. "I'm not going to do anything for you. Think of it as payback if you want. But I'm done with the two of you. You've plotted and planned to have myself and Conard killed. You've also tried to blow up a lot of people in the place where he was—"

"They were all retards too, Clare." She looked at her mom. "Everyone but you knows that they don't have real feelings. They're just stupid people that have to be taken care of all the

174

time. Haven't you wanted to just take out a gun and blow his head off, just to get him to go away?"

"No, I've never once had that feeling about him. You? Then yes, all the time, but not my brother." Her mom looked shocked. "What bothers you about him? Because he's different? He is, thankfully, nothing like the two of you. Is it because he takes a little longer to learn something? Good for him. He knows a great deal more than the two of you do."

"How the heck do you figure that?" Dad looked at Mom, then at her. "Clare, I hate to say this to you, but what if that baby of yours is like him? Surely you can't think to keep it. Not with all that money you have. Speaking of which, we're going to have to revise our list that we need. I mean, now that you have billions, you can part with enough to keep us in good shape. I was thinking about ten grand a month, and you make the all the payments on the cars as well as a lovely home for us. But we're going to need a— Why is it that you keep bobbing up and down like that? Sit down, Clare. I'm not nearly finished with you."

"But I'm finished with you." She gathered her things, glad now that she'd not brought them the cookies. "Don't have them contact me again. I won't come here again. And you're not to bother my family either. If you do, then—"

"But we're your family." She told him not anymore. "Clare, I don't know what's come over you, but I won't have it. You come right back here and sit down. We're going to tell you our needs and you're going to get them for us. Your mother needs her treatments. Her face...well, just look at it. They're not giving her what she needs."

"You aren't giving me what I need either." Dad told her

that she had all the money she needed. "That's all you can think about, isn't it? Money. And what it can do for you. Believe it or not, there are other things that can be had, and it has nothing to do with how much is in your bank account."

"We have no money in our account, Clare. That's what we've been trying to tell you all along. Now, as I was saying, you need to put some money in our account. Things cost money here. And it's entirely too much, if you ask me. I have a plan to supply treats and stuff to people in jail so that they don't have to pay those prices. Of course, I'll need some startup money. After that, I'll be making a profit in no time." She asked him if he was going to pay her back for the startup money. "Don't be ridiculous, Clare. Why would I do that? Anyway, after we're making a profit, I'll need to expand. A bigger truck, a new one, not one that has any miles on it. Also, it'll need to have air. I don't want to melt with the candies and such. When can you make this happen? Sooner rather than later, I'm thinking."

"When you get out of prison, if you still want this, then it's yours." Dad was all smiles then, and she just shook her head. "You do know that you're never going to get out of here at any age when you're going to want to do this, correct? Not to mention, you can't get a loan with having a record. And then there is the added fact that you won't have an address, nor a bank account. It's just not in the cards."

"Honey, I hate to keep beating a dead horse here, but you have money. Therefore, we have it too. Why can't you get that through your thick head? As I was saying too, we're going to need for you to make this all go away. As you pointed out.... Wait, I won't need a loan, so it'll not matter about that part.

And you'll put money in our account for us, right?" She said no. "You're saying that now, but once I have this all down on paper, you'll want to help us. It'll be the greatest moneymaker that I've ever had."

"You mean like robbing Mr. Boone of his diamonds? Or how about you killing off yourself in a fake death to have the insurance come to you? I wasn't able to let that one go on, so I canceled it, along with Mr. Boone's." Mom told her she was being unfair. "Unfair? You took out a policy on Conrad so that when you had the Sherman Oaks blow up, you'd get millions of dollars."

"That would have worked, too, had you just kept out of it. Why did you take him out of that place? It was the best place for all of us. Clare, you are forever putting your nose in where it doesn't belong." Dad shook his head. "Well, that's water under the bridge now. I forgive you for costing us a lot of money. This is why you're going to do this for us. Because you've messed with our well-laid plans from before."

She stood up this time and turned to look at them when they shouted at her to return. "Don't call me again. Don't have anyone else do it either. I'm finished with the two of you. You can both rot in hell, where I suspect that you'll end up, for all I care about you. As parents, you have sucked donkey balls. As humans? Well, I'm better off with people who aren't humans than I am with either of you as any part of my life." She went out the door but went back to see them once more. "Fuck you both."

The ride home was done with her crying so hard that she had to pull over twice to get herself under control. She did speak to Owen twice, and he told her that he'd come to get her, but she said that she needed a few minutes. Pulling off the road again, she wrapped her hands around the place where she thought their child was.

"I love you. And every day for the rest of our lives, I'm going to make sure that you know that. I'm going to be there every time you ask me to be. Even times when you don't think you'll need me. I'm going to be your mom, not your mother, and no matter what happens to you, I will love you with all my being and never ever expect you to do things like my parents did." She grinned a little. "By the way, as of today, they don't exist anymore. You have no grandparents on my side of the family. Someday I might tell you about them, but don't count on it. They're horrible people."

Clare spoke to Sara Jane all the way home, telling her about her dad about her uncles. "You'll love Conrad. He'll be the best friend you'll ever have. And your biggest champion." More things about her new family came to her as she told her all about Sara and Kelley. The things they were going to do.

When she got home she felt amazing. Like she had done more than just cut the fat out of her life, as Kelley called it, but had become a new person because of being able to say the things she had to them. Clare was happy, happier than she'd ever thought possible.

~*~

Xander was still writing when he heard Addie come in. The hotel they were in was lovely, but it wasn't nearly as much fun when she wasn't there. When she joined him at the desk that had been set up for him, he held her in his arms and asked how things had gone.

"Very well." He didn't want a lot of information on her

178

work. In fact, after her telling him what he'd need to know about some of the shit she did, he decided that he didn't want to know any of it. Like why she was considered the best. It was enough for him to know that what she was doing was a great service, and he was happy with that.

"You and I have dinner plans tonight." Addie yawned. "After that, we're supposed to spend the night at the White House for a memorial for Mrs. Baker."

Candis Baker had died five days ago when she contracted the flu and never recovered. What had really happened, Xander didn't know, nor did he want to, but he supposed that it had nothing to do with any kind of virus, and more to do with one of the weapons on Addie's body.

"Ben told me that we didn't have to go. He said that it's going to be hard enough trying to keep a straight face when someone tells him how sorry they are for his loss. I never dreamed she was that deep into selling off government information." No one had, it seemed. "And the fact that she'd gotten her husband elected says a great deal for her power over people. What do you suppose the country would say if they found out?"

"For Ben? I'd say they were thrilled to death about him being there. There is a lot to be said for the health care being so good here. That people on welfare have to get a job to receive their help. And the fact that the economy is booming again, all good in his favor. If he runs again, I'm sure that they'll elect him." She yawned again, and he picked her up to carry her to their room. "You take a nap, and I'll wake you in enough time for us to have dinner. All right?"

"Sure. Oh, before I forget, I'm pregnant."

Saying sure to her, he left her to rest. When it finally hit him what she'd said, he turned around and went back to her. But she was asleep, snoring softly while her body was limp with exhaustion.

He sat at his desk for the next twenty or so minutes, thinking about having a child. Penny was going to be so happy that she'd have a fit about having a sister or brother. He wondered if Addie could tell what it was, but decided if she didn't, he'd not tell her. But knowing her, she more than likely wouldn't take the entire nine months, wouldn't gain an ounce, and she'd be carrying the baby in one hand while fighting with the other. Laughing, he went back to his work.

The studio had asked him who he had wanted to play certain parts in the movie. He didn't have any idea, but they had nicely sent him a list of possible candidates. Some of these were big names.

He worked until about midnight, going in to Addie once and seeing that she was still sleeping. Stripping down, he moved to curl around her, and was glad when she wrapped her body around his. As soon as she sighed heavily and snored softly, he closed his own eyes. It was going to be a long day tomorrow. They were going house hunting for this area.

They had already booked their trip overseas. It was going to be a honeymoon for them, and after a few days of soaking up the sun, his family was going to join them. It was going to be the best cover he could think of, and they'd have a blast while they were at it. He'd been doing shopping too, at every place they went since leaving home ten days ago.

Penny was coming tomorrow. She was going to fly over with Mom and Dad, then they were going to look for ornaments. Dad had enlisted the help of Penny to find them for her own tree, but if the number of boxes coming in were any indication, he was pretty sure they had enough for several trees, but he didn't care. It was the first Christmas for a great many things this year.

"You're thinking hard again." He kissed her, and she smiled. "Okay, if that's what you were thinking about, then you can think hard like that all the time."

"Are you really going to have our baby?" She nodded at him. "When are you due? I'm assuming that it'll be in about nine months, or is that wrong too?"

"Nine hours." She turned to her back, her belly growing, and he nearly had a heart attack. "You are so gullible, Xander. However did you make it through life believing every word people say to you?"

He tickled her mercilessly, then laughed with her. Life with this woman would never be like the rest of the family — she was going to keep him on his toes forever. Kissing her again, he held her to him with his hand over her still flat belly.

"I don't know if I'll be a good mom or not. I never had one." He looked down at her and told her he was sorry. "Yeah, no biggie. I never expected to have a child, much less a person in my life."

"I'm glad you have me in your life and that we're going to have a baby." He kissed her belly now and laid his head on her. "I talked to Owen. He said that Clare went to see her parents today. I guess she cried all the way home, but feels better."

"She's not going to be one to mess with, I don't think. Clare is stronger than any of the rest of them." He asked her why. "She's had to be. Those parents are not ones that could be easily circumvented when necessary. I'm betting that at any given time, she had to fight them tooth and nail to keep Conrad safe. Did I tell you that she found out that they had done that hurt to her, not Conrad, when they had him put away?"

"Owen told me. He's going to the auction house again next month after the holidays. He told me that he's going to sell off most of the tea cups, that they've decided that they only want a few of them. And you know what he's doing with the gems he's found." She nodded, and he heard her belly growl. "Why don't we go out and find some place open and have a feast?"

"Chinese." Xander agreed. "With a lot of appetizers. And soup. Hot and sour, with those little crunchy things in them. Oh, and something spicy. I want—"

"Why don't I just order the menu?" At her nod, he shook his head. "Or we could learn to pace ourselves." His phone was ringing, and he went to get it. Addie said she'd take care of the food.

When he went back to the living area, she was on the phone. Opening his computer, he pulled up the houses that had been sent to him by the White House. He was still getting his mind wrapped around the fact that his wife was a hitman for the CIA and worked directly with the president.

When she got off, she came to where he was and glanced over his shoulder. "Ben just called and said that he was looking at that house." He opened the house folder on his computer to look at the rooms. "Wow, don't you think that's kind of big? I mean, what the hell will we do with nine bedrooms?"

"I think we'll have family around a lot." She said she'd not thought of that. "Yeah, I'm sure that he did. Anyway, I love the office area. There are two of them. See?" She said that she'd take the basement over, for all the equipment that she'd need. "I was hoping for a kind of gym down there. I mean, as a writer, I don't want to be getting fat."

They were both laughing when he looked the house over again with her on his lap. The house was nice but would need a little tweaking. Not just new appliances, but they had to have a good security system, as well as a phone and Internet that would be off the grid. Again, having a wife like his, it was going got be different than other wives.

"I think we should take it. To be honest with you, I'm sick of being in this hotel all the time with round the clock guards. I want real life things going on, like a backyard barbeque." She asked him if they did that at home. "Yes—it doesn't matter the weather either. We enjoy the out of doors."

"I do as well, but I don't get to it much. I mean, I'm hoping I will now, but I don't work as much as I used to either." He nodded at her and put in an offer for the house. In seconds it came back as sold. "I guess we missed it."

"Yeah, we'll keep looking." When someone knocked at the door, he went to get it as she pouted about the house. "My first pick and I missed it. You think we should just buy them all?"

"No, I do not." Xander opened the door to see four men standing there with bags. "Honey, how much food did you order? It looks like— Please tell me you did not order the menu. We can't eat all this."

"Yes, I did, I told you I was, and we got a discount." She

took two of the bags of still hot food while he tipped the men. "Oh, and invite our security team in—there will be enough for them too."

They ate with gusto, and he was pleased that they had few leftovers. He was cleaning up as Addie showed their guys out, and someone came to the door again—a special courier for the president. Addie was laughing when she shut the door behind her.

"We have the house. Ben bought it for us while we were trying to decide if we wanted fried or white rice." Xander said that was never a question. "You know what I mean. But we have the house. Now guess what we get to do? We get to furnish it. Yay."

Hopefully they'd get to do that too, before Ben did. Clean up was easy, and they were settled in front of the computer again a few minutes after that. Bellies full, they yawned a great deal but found some pieces that they wanted to look at tomorrow. Things were looking up for them, and they could not wait until they had their home ready to live in.

XANDER

Chapter 12

"What do you think?" Xander looked at the spread of food and smiled. Addie laughed as she continued. "Yeah, that's what I was thinking too. They're going to think we're nuts and have to order pizzas as soon as they get home."

"I doubt they'll wait that long if they think this is crap. But, in our defense, this was Dad's idea." She nodded and left him in the dining room to get more plates. They had more than enough, but he let her fuss. It was sort of funny.

The day before they were all to meet at his parents' house for the first of seven dinners for the holidays, Dad had brought out a hat. It was filled with countries that he wanted to try. It took them a long explanation, finally from Mom, to figure out that he wanted to try foods. They all thought it was his way of figuring out where Mom might like to go on a long cruise. It was brilliant, and Caleb bitched for an hour that he'd not thought of it. Xander and Addie's was Japanese.

They had had to go to the Internet several times after that

night. Grayson complained a great deal, but Xander thought he was having a blast. And Mom and Dad had told them if they didn't make it, that was fine, it had been sort of sprung on them. When he told Grayson that, he looked like he might be upset.

"I'm a chef of the highest order. I do not fail my families. We shall have the best damned Japanese dinner of all time, or I shall quit my job." Addie told him to do the best that he could. "I always do, madam. And have a glass of juice, please. The baby needs all it can get."

They'd not told anyone about the baby yet, so they were still standing there when he returned with not just one, but two glasses of juice, one for each of them. Then he closed his mouth. Cheeky bastard.

Today they were having everything they could think of. And since no one had any idea, that he knew of, what the things were, he'd made little stick labels. This was to tell them what it was as well as what would be in it. He wasn't taking any chances with his first meal here.

When his family arrived, they had gifts. He'd forgotten about that—a token, Mom called it, for the house holding the meal. But Addie had remembered and passed out her little gifts to everyone, and smiled a great deal as they looked confused with them. Each of them had a baby item, from diaper pens to powder.

"We're having a baby." No one moved except to look at him. Addie laughed as she went on to explain. "You couldn't tell either, could you? Good. It's nice to know that we can pull one over on you once in a while. I don't know if anyone has ever told you this, but you're the nosiest bunch that I've ever seen."

After laughing and hugging everyone, they proceeded to the dining room. From his vantage point at the table, he could see that it was a strange lot. He also noticed that all his little signs were gone. When asked about it, Grayson said it was intimidating and he had taken them off. Oh well, they were in for some explaining. Grayson cleared his throat to quiet the room.

"We have gone a little overboard in our selection tonight. But we thought, with so many of you, that it might also not be enough. For those of you who wish to be chickens and not try some of the food, I have laid the house phone there, so that you might order in. Pizza is the only thing delivered this far from town." His cook had just shamed his family into trying new things. And Xander loved it.

There were several kinds of sushi, something that Xander had liked when they were having sample night a few days ago. The rare tuna was his favorite. There were other items folded over the seasoned rice too. Vegetables, nori or seaweed, and fish. He loved this part and was surprised that his dad did as well. Everyone had their favorites, and he was glad that they were trying the chopsticks as well. The wasabi wasn't well received, he didn't think, but it was an acquired taste. And Penny loved the spicy hotness of it.

Tempura was brought out in smaller plates—it was to be served hot. There was chicken for the most part, but Grayson had also made vegetables and fruit with the batter. Xander didn't care for this part of the meal. He thought that it was a waste of fresh food. But Addie could eat it by the plateful.

They had udon noodles, as well as ones made from

buckwheat. All sorts of delicate little teas were there to try, all of them served in the tea cups that Owen had lent him. And in the end, he'd give each person the cups as his token for when they came to his home next week.

For the desserts, they'd hired a friend of Addie's to come and make them. They were beautiful, almost too pretty to eat. Addie told him that they made an art of their desserts so that the meal will be more memorable. He thought it was that all on its own.

"Son, I have to tell you, I was a little afeard of what you might be bringing out for us. I noticed that there was a bit of ham sammiches in the kitchen there. None of us had to resort to them. You did good." His dad hugged him. "Another grandbaby. I can't believe my blessings, I just can't. All these babies here now, they was more than I ever dreamed possible for an old man like me."

"Dad, you do know that we didn't have children just for you?"

He shook his head and Penny came to hug her grandda. She was calling them all by family names now — uncles, aunts as well as grandma and grandpa. She even called Harley and Conrad her brothers.

They were very protective of her too. Even Harley would walk right beside her when they were out for a walk. Just yesterday he'd had to save her. It had been serious but funny too. The snake was no more afraid of her than she was of it, but Harley scared it away for her with rocks. Dominic had taught him to stay away from them at the camp.

All in all he thought it was perfect. And since they were finished with the meal, they had planned on putting up their tree. But Penny, ever a bright light on any day, had decided that since theirs was the first to go up, they needed to have the family do it. So, they were all invited to stay and snacks were set out for them as they enjoyed the activity of decorating the tree. And with the beautiful ornaments that her and the family had found, they had enough to go around for everyone to help.

Tradition was out the window with their tree that was in the grand hallway. They had done a lot of traveling lately, and would continue to do so. Every place they went, Penny and Addie would find something to hang on the tree. It didn't have to be an ornament, but anything that reminded them of where they had gone. And when they didn't find it to be hangable, they asked someone to fix it for them. He especially loved the little snow globes that had had a glass hook put on the top so that they could hang them.

The doorbell rang about ten minutes after the tree was as done as it could be. There wasn't a branch on the ten-foot tree that didn't have something hanging from it. The colored lights were festive, as well as the beautiful garland that had been found in the bottom of one of the boxes left behind by Rayne's family. A few ornaments as well.

Grayson handed out the boxes that had arrived so that everyone could open them as he read the missive, his word of the day, to each of them. The gifts were from the president.

"Hello, my favorite family. Enclosed you will find a little of DC from me. It has taken me some time to gather them all, but I finally got them for you. Enjoy them for your tree, and know that you will each receive a new ornament when it is made for Christmas for the rest of your lives. Thank you for all your support and friendship. Love you all, Ben."

"You know they've been doing this every year since nineteen eighty-one. But these here, they're from whenever they did one. My goodness, Xander, this is a very expensive gift. I don't know what to say about all this." Dad knew the strangest bits of history, and since he'd been to the White House, he knew a good deal more about that place. "Oh, my goodness."

Each of the ornaments had been hand painted and crafted. There was a note with each of them, telling of the designer as well as who had painted it for them. The cards with them, each a blank card with Benjamin Baker scrawled over it, had also been by his own hand, and meant so much more as he had put the recipient's name on each of the cards. Xander was as touched as his mom was.

"These need their own tree. I think I might have one." He took off to the basement to find the wire tree that he'd unearthed when looking for Christmas lights. Coming back up, he found his family in the living room with the second tree, this one closer to the fireplace. He set down the wired eight-foot tree with curls at the end of each branch, which seemed to be the perfect place for the special ornaments.

As Penny hung them for them, she read what year it had been designed and who had done it. His favorite was the car with the tree hanging from the back. There were others too. Wives of the presidents. There were also candid shots of them with their wives. His mom had loved the Kennedy one, and Dad, of course, enjoyed the one with the horse drawn carriage.

He knew that they had to leave day after tomorrow. Addie had two jobs to do, neither of which, as far as he knew, had anything to do with her killing anyone. But she did have to check on the security of a building, as well as go to the camp that the president went to for the holidays and make sure that there weren't any issues. He was going to spend two days with his daughter and wife there, just because it was empty.

When his family left the tree was finished, both of them, and the mess had been cleaned up. He and his little family went to the living room to watch some television. He was both shocked and sort of glad when he heard on the news that both Ava and Con Macintosh were finally on their way to prison. He watched several times while they shouted to the camera for Clare to come and get them.

"We should invite them to go with us." Xander asked Penny what she was talking about. "Aunt Clare and Uncle Owen. They'd like to get away, I'm betting. And Conrad too. We can have lobster, like you said we could. And I know that I don't know how to eat them, but Conrad said that it's easy once you get the legs cut off."

"How does Conrad know how to eat a lobster?" She told him. "Oh, well, I guess he would understand that, working in a restaurant like he had. Yes, if they want to come with us, I'm sure no one would mind. We can have a weekend full of walking on the beach and having fun."

"It'll be cold, right? Too cold for the water, I guess." He told her it was. "Well, we can go shell hunting and have some good food. I can write a report on it for extra credit too."

She didn't need the extra credit. Since they'd put her in private school, due to the job that Addie did, she'd been excelling. Reading at a senior level, she also excelled in math and in French. Spending a couple of weeks listening to videos on the Internet had been fun and educational for them all. And since that had worked out so well, she'd been taking courses on learning as many languages as she could. He loved every bit of her enthusiasm. And her.

When Caleb's boys came over a few hours later, to spend the night and to go fishing in the morning, Addie and he lounged on the couch. It was going to be a long day tomorrow. First of all they had to pack up, then they had to make arrangements to get things delivered to DC for the work she had to do.

He never asked and decided that was the best way to go about this. He wasn't squeamish, but he thought that he might look at her differently if he knew what she did when she left to go to work. Perhaps not differently, but he would worry more.

Chapter 13

Dominic loved the outdoors, even the cooler weather that they were having now. But it was much too cold for the kids at the camp, even with the large fire they had burning. He tossed a couple more logs on the fire and decided that it was pointless to keep it going. The buses would be here soon, and they would all be gone for the rest of the year. He glanced over at the table full of Christmas gifts and smiled. This year was the first one he'd been able to do something like this.

The money that he'd been given by Mr. Cartwright had gone a long way in making things better for the children here. Just last month he'd been able to replace the furnace that had been going bad for months now. So instead of just having heat on the cooler mornings, they also had air conditioning for the hot days of summer, which even the people cooking loved. Dominic moved toward the kitchen area now.

"Mr. Winchester?" He turned, thinking it was one of the volunteers again, just ready to tell them to call him Dom, when the man smiled. "You don't know me. I'm Mr. Burt of Burt and Burt."

"It's very nice to meet you. As you know, I'm Dominic. Everyone around here just calls me Dom. It's easier for them." He nodded as if he knew. "If you're waiting on someone to go home with you, I'm afraid without written prior permission, I can't let you take anyone. Not while in our care."

"No, no. I don't want to do that. I would, however, like a word with you. You see, I've been sent here." Dominic nodded and waited. "When the children are all gone, then you and I will talk. Can I keep the fire going? It's been a long while since I've been free to stand near a fire as I am now. Warmed, I guess you could call it."

"Yes, all right."

He turned when he heard the buses pulling in and then looked at the man. But he was already at the fire, tossing logs onto it from the pile. Dominic shook his head. He could have sworn that the man sparkled.

The kids were both ready to go home to see their families and wanting to stay. He wanted them to do both as well. Handing each of their caretakers their package and then an envelope for each of the volunteers, he had the first bus loaded in no time. The second one didn't go as quickly, but he waited while the young man who didn't want to leave at all gathered himself some control.

"Come on now, Davey, don't you want to see your cat? I'm sure that she's missed you." Davey was non-verbal but he could speak ASL. They taught American Sign language to all the students on some level, and this young man was no different. "I don't remember your cat's name. What is it?"

194

He spelled out Skittles. That was it. A great name for a domestic cat, but not so much for a shifter, he'd bet. And Davey was a cat who had no control over his other self. So, his sister, the Skittles in this circumstance, was helping him be calm at home.

It happened, sometimes, that a shifter would have a handicapped child. Not because of a birth defect, if they were both pure bloods, but due to a faulty cord or perhaps a fall or something. It made it difficult for those children to have any kind of normalcy to their lives. That was why, three times a year, he had a camp now for shifter children and adults. But to Dominic, they were all children.

Getting Davey on the bus was made harder by the fact that his cat came out. The big cat was just like his counterpart — mentally handicapped, but gentle for the most part. As soon as he figured out that they were both all right, he became himself again and was redressed. It was smooth sailing after that.

Five brand new buses, all thanks to Harley's dad and the foundation that he'd set up for them. There were blankets now too, plenty enough to send home, with their names on them, as well as what was wrong with them along the bottom.

It was a safety measure. The name of the child, whether or not they could talk, and the severity of their disability was imprinted on the blanket. It would help them if they were in an accident. There was also a code, as well as a phone number that they could call to get in touch with the family. He loved that part most of all.

The man was still by the fire when he was able to go to him. The fire had died down a little, but it was still warm,

195

and the wood looked as if he'd never touched it. Dominic was exhausted after this week and was sure that he'd just imagined the lack of wood being used.

"Mr. Winchester, my name is Shamus Burt. Everyone calls me Sham. Like the pretty little clover in the spring." Dominic took his hand and felt the small tingle of magic. "You're a good man—has anyone but your family realized that?"

"Every person that works here is a good person, Mr. Burt. You said you had to talk to me. I don't mean to be rude, but I'm exhausted. Why, earlier I thought you were sparkling. That's how tired I am." He nodded and grinned, taking off his hat. "My goodness. You look just like a leprechaun."

He didn't just change in appearance, but he got smaller too—like only a foot or so tall, when before removing his hat, he'd been nearly as tall as Dominic. Rubbing his eyes, trying to make himself see what he was actually seeing, he smiled when the man laughed.

"That's good. Because I am one. A good leprechaun too. I've come to talk to you about your camp. You've— Something wrong?" The red-haired man stood up, then sat down. It was then that he noticed that he was sporting a red mustache and that he had freckles all over his nose. And when he pulled out a pipe, Dominic didn't just sit to the ground, but slipped off the seat to it in one motion. "I'm a wee bit too much for you, aren't I, sir?"

"Yes, a wee bit too much is about right. What do you want with me? I've not seen a pot of gold around. I've not trapped you into anything, and I don't remember ever picking a flower without smelling it." Burt laughed. "Yes, I know all the rules of the wee people. My mother's aunt was married to one."

"Yes, so she was. But I'm here as a friend of that same uncle. He's sending me here to talk to you, and to make sure you have what you need to keep the wee ones here happy. We're coming to help you." Dominic shook his head. He wasn't sure if he was saying no or that he was shaking lose the cobwebs, but he did shake himself. "You'll be fine in a bit there. Would you like a wee dram of whiskey? Might cut through the confusion."

"What does my uncle want with me? And no, I don't drink. It does very little good to my kind." He nodded and took a drink of something from his pocket. "While I'm pretty sure that I'm dreaming, taking a nap here on the bench with the fire dying down, I don't understand how it is you can help us."

"You see, we see them here. When they're out and about, we turn them back, the wee ones—back to the camp when they slip by you. They don't wander far, but when they do, we help them. And in return, they help us. Did you know the touch of a wee one like them can bring all kind of coin to a man like me self?" Dominic said that he'd not heard that one. "Well, we've a pot of gold for you to use. And as I said, our help."

"The pot of gold might be useful. I've used the last of my money buying up the rest of the acreage around us." He was kidding, but as soon as the pot, bigger than a car, was in front of him, Dominic stood up to look inside. He was loving this dream—too bad that it wasn't real. He might have to take out a loan for the next couple of seasons. "This is a lot of gold. I don't understand why you'd be giving me this. Or for that matter, if I'm dreaming or not."

The pinch to his ass startled him, and he turned to see who had done it. The wee little woman moved to stand next to Burt, and they both held hands.

"To see if I'm awake, I guess." The woman nodded, and it was then that he noticed that she was handicapped as well. "May I be permitted to ask?"

"She fell down a well when she was no more than a babe. Not breathing hurt her mind, but she's a good girl and we care for each other. Maggie is my sister. And your uncle is our king. Good King O'Reilly Shamus James. He has been since he met with your aunt. But now that he's taking on so much more, he's delegated me to come to talk to you. To give you some help, as I said."

"Am I really awake?" Sham asked if he wanted Maggie to pinch him again. "No, that won't be necessary. What does this plan of yours involve? I mean, how will you be able to help me? Besides the money. This is real, right?"

"Oh yes, very real. And the fact that I've brought it to you, once you touch it, it'll be more into what you can handle. Gold, as you know, is heavy." Dominic felt like he was on one of the carnival rides that took you around and around, and then let you off while you were still spinning in the head. "You'll be right as rain, Dom, I promise you."

"This money, what's it for?" He told him. "Why would he want me to buy more land? We have more than we can use now."

"You do. Here. But not where you might do more good. A bigger city perhaps. And the funding that you have now will only be a drop in the bucket compared to what you'll have in way of help from other clans. And there will be clans helping you gather the land up too. With houses and buildings. No more furnaces going out either." Dominic asked what the catch was. "Catch? No catch. Just use the money for the little ones here and around the world, and the rest will be easy. You must use it for them. You understand?"

"I would never steal from the funding we get." He said he knew that, but he did have to say it. "And this money, it'll be there for all kinds of things? Like new buildings for the wee ones, as you call them? The blankets that we send home with them?"

"Oh aye. That and more, my sir." Dominic didn't know why he was having such a fanciful dream, but he wasn't going to complain. But he did know that he was going to be sore, if he was indeed sleeping on the bench. "You'd not be sleeping, my lord. You're as awake as I be."

"Yes, all right." Dominic touched one of the coins and felt the magic of it all the way to his ears. But when he looked at the coin that he'd touched it was green money, cash that he could use for anything. He looked at Sham. "This is strange — you know that, right? I mean, who believes in leprechauns? Who believes in pots of gold?"

"You'd be doing that, sir, or I'd not be here with you. You must believe, a little at least." Dominic nodded. "You're remembering, aren't you?"

"Yes. When I was a little boy, no more than about two, I remember seeing one of the people like you. I was in my playpen, a fenced off area, while my mom hung out the wash. And suddenly this little man, a wee little man no bigger than me, came into my area because the cat was chasing him."

"Aye. And you saved me, didn't you, young Dominic?

199

Scared that cat off and let me run away. I've never forgotten you. Never will, either." Dominic shook his head again and stared at the man. "You'll be fine as rain in the morning now. You go on to your home, and in the morning, we'll talk again."

Dominic found himself sitting on his couch at his home. Sitting there, he thought about his dream and wondered what the hell he'd eaten today. Getting up, he stretched and heard his back pop. It had been doing that a lot lately, so he knew that he'd fallen asleep again where he shouldn't have.

Just as he was headed up to his bed, he reached into his pocket to place his keys on the table. When he tossed them there, he nearly screamed.

There it was. A gold coin. And on the face of it was the very same little leprechaun that had been talking to him. On the flip side was his Uncle O'Reilly. Christ, he needed to find Gabe and have his head examined. And he would, first thing in the morning.

~*~

"Aye, and you talked to him? Gave him the message?" Sham said that he had and that Dom had touched the pot. "Did he ask?"

"Nay, he didn't." They had had a bet, the two of them. King O'Reilly had said that he'd not use the money for nary a thing but the school. Sham had thought he'd buy himself a trinket. He hadn't done either, but made his way home. Might have been his magic too, but now that he'd met the young man, he knew him to be as honest as the day was long.

The question that they all thought he might ask, with the exception of King O'Reilly, was what the money would bring him. They had nothing for him if he did that. But like his true king, he didn't ask. And Sham was glad that he'd been wrong.

"When do you speak to him again? Soon? You think I should go too, to have a word or two with him?" Sham asked him what he'd say that he couldn't. "Nothing. But I have a need for him, Sham. Him and his mate. She's not here yet, thankfully. She's a temper on her. But when she comes, there will be hell to pay. We know it."

"Yes, she's a fine temper, that girl. But we made a promise. We're to keep it." O'Reilly said that he'd do it, but he hated to be in pain. "She'll do it too, that girl. I'm a scared of her, if you want the truth."

"Yes, me too. She's as fiery as her hair, that one is." Charlotte O'Farrell—just the mention of her name made him shiver in his boots. "When are you going to tell her?"

"Me? I'm not telling her a blessed thing about this. You do it." Sham nearly fell over his big feet trying to back away from his king. "You go ahead and tell her the plan when she comes along. I'll pay you."

"Nay, you will not pay me, and you want to know why you won't be parting with your own gold? Because I'll not do it. She'll hurt me. Cut me to ribbons with her tongue, that one will. You cannot even...I cannot be believing that you'd ask me such a thing. Me being your own brother and all."

"But you like her." He told him that he didn't like her enough to be murdered by her. "Leave her a note."

"You leave her a note. But you'd best be signing your death warrant too. She's going to blister you with her words, see if she doesn't."

There wasn't a person in their clan that didn't have a fear, a good fear, of Charlie. Charlie was a good woman, full of humor when she wasn't angry. Which by his estimation was most of the time, but she could cook and bake. Her gardens always looked the neatest, and there wasn't a child that didn't love her with all their hearts, until they got old enough to piss the darling off. Which really wasn't that easy.

She cared not for stupid people. Sadly, she thought all people over the age of about two hundred, his age and then some, were stupid. She didn't suffer fools either, and made sure that she was around when they fell upon their faces after she told them this or that wouldn't work. Not to tell them she told them so, but to pick them up, dust them off, and make them do it right. Her way. Also, Charlie had no troubles telling you that you were wrong. Not once in all the times that he'd been subject to her tongue lashing had she ever hurt him with a club. Her voice and words were bad enough. He would almost pity the young man to be her mate but for the fact that Charlie could and did love with all her heart. And that was as big as any pot of gold that he'd ever had.

"You think of what I must say to her." Sham said he wasn't going to be party to it. "That's what we'll do. Have a party."

The man was daft. His fear of talking to the young lass was making his head addled. And when he started planning this party, Sham started to walk away, making his way backwards without taking his eyes off the sad king who'd lost his mind.

"I've done no such thing." He'd forgotten that his brother could read his mind. "You'll help me plan this party, and while she's having herself a fine spirit or two, we'll tell her. From a distance. While our bags are packed, and the ship is pulling away."

"She'll find us. It won't matter."

He thought about young Charlie. She wasn't a terrible person, not like they were talking about her, not really. She did have a fine temper, and that red hair that was as natural to them as grass being green. Charlie was a magical as her mother had been, and a good leprechaun she'd been too. But she was also beautiful beyond compare.

A real beauty. Long red hair that curled up like someone had curled it for her. Ringlets, he thought them called. Lips as rosy as the flowers that bloomed year-round for them. A face that looked like she'd been soaking it in the creamiest milk for years, it was so soft and white. Eyes the color of the darkest of emeralds, and as hard too when she wanted them to be. He loved the girl, as most did, but she could turn on you in a moment and you'd wish that you didn't know her at all.

"Well, there's no hope for it, I guess. We'll have to send her away." Sham thought he'd missed something, had missed where they were sending her to and why. But O'Reilly spoke again, and he nearly sagged with relief. "We'll send her into the world of the big people and see that she falls for our young Dominic. We all know that without him being born and his children being born, then none of us would be able to survive."

"Now don't be going all dramatic, O'Reilly. He saved my life and in turn yours, but the rest — well, that's just a bunch of malarkey and you know it. He'll be what we need. Or not. But whatever happens when he helps us, it's the way it should have been." Nodding, O'Reilly told him he was right. "Of course I am. And to show you how right I am, I'll tell Charlie when she gets here that you need to talk to her."

He was nearly home before he no longer heard his brother screaming at him. It had been a good joke, telling him that last part before leaving. Taking a turn at the little road he was on, he walked by Dominic's home, to see that he'd made it to bed all right.

Dominic had saved him that day. Not only that, but he'd in turn saved his children. That wasn't a joke. Had he been killed that day, his children would not have come to pass. His wife would have not borne him any sons. The boys that he had now, all eighteen of them, would not have been able to have him grandchildren, one of which was in the big people world.

"Aye, my Donnie is out there now, making us money and investing in our future. But it's the one we have right now that needs the work most. And Dominic will make that come to pass." He looked at the big book, the one that he'd been in charge of since he'd been old enough to carry it. The Book of Leprechaun. And someday, Dominic would take care of it for them. For not just this clan, but all of them.

Opening the pages at random, he saw the names there. The dates of their births, their children's births too. And deaths. More and more they were dying off. And for the simple reason that no one believed in them.

There were funny jokes about them. People would talk about the pretty rainbow that would lead them right to them, but no one bothered to look anymore. No one cared that the leprechauns were dying because no one believed in their magic.

It was happenstance that had him touch one of the wee ones at Dominic's camp. They gave him such energy that he'd touched all the wee ones that came around. He felt younger than he had in decades. Better too, no more aches and moans. All because of a wee one seeing him.

"Harley, my man, you have given us more than you can ever be repaid for." He laughed when he thought of the antics of the wee one. Such a name for them, but that's what they all called them. Wee ones were going to be able to save the leprechauns, if only they could get Dominic to talk others into believing in them.

As he made his way home, he could smell the bread baking from his oven. His lady wife would have him a sup that would be better than any large people ever ate. He'd have a fried potato, a green bean cut just so. There would be a beet sliced for the two of them, and a glass of the juice that she'd squeeze with her very hands. Mildred was the best of wives — the best cook too, so far as he could tell. Except for Charlie.

Charlie had been born on a stormy night. The walls around her parents' home were so close to falling in that everyone worried that the wee babe would be swept away. But she was in her little crib when they found her the next morning. She and her blanket, the one that she wore upon her head even now, were all that was left of her home. Both of her parents had died that night, never to be found by man nor beast.

She'd grown up right before their eyes, the child, to become a woman. Never asking for help when she could do it on her own. Learning to cook and to sew gave her coin enough until she was old enough to gather her own. Then she bought not just a house in the clan, but one in the large people world as well. Becoming a cook there too, so that she could support herself and those around her. Her goodness was as legendary as her temper.

There was little about the girl that he didn't respect or love. Charlie was smart too. Smarter than a large person about so many things. She could also guide a slip of a boat, fish with the best of them, and again, cook her own meals like she'd done it all her life.

Charlie was also able to bring newborns into the world. Her job, this one, was slowing, and it was her that had first come to him about it—that there weren't as many babes being born as there had been. So, O'Reilly sent her to the other clans, to see what they were doing. If they were having a slowdown of children as well. So far, the news hadn't been good.

Babes born in the cities were the worst numbers. Babes in the country were better, but not by a big margin. They needed believers. And short of showing themselves and getting caught, there was little they could do. Until they saw Dominic and the blue glow of kindness around him.

The wee ones were his children. It mattered little, Sham thought, that some were older than him in years and some younger by only months. He loved them all, like they were his own children. When they found out that he'd spent his own money on gifts this year for them all, they knew that they'd found the right man for the job—the job of marrying their Charlie and having children.

"Do you think she'll be all right with him? She'll not kill him? She's a powerful temper, that Charlie." Sham agreed with Mildred, but told her that he'd seen it. "Aye, you told me that first night. But I can worry for him, can't I? When you spoke to him tonight, I could tell that he wasn't believing. He thought himself asleep."

"He did, but he'll be all right when I speak to him again." He'd told the young man that he'd speak to him on the morrow, but it would be later, much later. "When Charlie returns, we'll have a sit down and tell her what's what."

Mildred huffed and asked him if he had her enough coin to live on when he was gone. Sham had to laugh. They all loved Charlie, to be sure, but there wasn't a one of them that wasn't terrified that she'd turn her temper onto them.

Before You Go...

HELP AN AUTHOR

write a review

THANK YOU!

Share your voice and help guide other readers to these wonderful books. Even if it's only a line or two your reviews help readers discover the author's books so they can continue creating stories that you'll love. Login to your favorite retailer and leave a review. Thank you.

AWARD WINNING, BESTSELLING AUTHOR

Kathi Barton, winner of the Pinnacle Book Achievement award as well as a best-selling author on Amazon and All Romance books, lives in Nashport, Ohio with her husband Paul. When not creating new worlds and romance, Kathi and her husband enjoy camping and going to auctions. She can also be seen at county fairs with her husband who is an artist and potter.

Her muse, a cross between Jimmy Stewart and Hugh Jackman, brings her stories to life for her readers in a way that has them coming back time and again for more. Her favorite genre is paranormal romance with a great deal of spice. You can visit Kathi online and drop her an email if you'd like. She loves hearing from her fans. aaronskiss@gmail.com.

Follow Kathi on her blog: http://kathisbartonauthor.blogspot.com/